The Tide Turns
Omega Chronicles 2

Artemis Milchon

AVALERION BOOKS INC.
Miami, Florida
avalerionbooks.com

Other Books By Artemis Milchon

Omega Chronicles

 THE LAST DRAGON

The Omega Clan Lords were sent to find the keys to free their world ...

Sally has never felt truly wanted. Not by family, friends, or the few men who ever took notice of her. But a single night out changes her life forever. She is abducted from a bar into a world she couldn't have imagined, and there she meets Drake, a gorgeous stranger with a mysterious past. As she falls under his spell, she must confront every insecurity she's ever had about herself. But Drake has much more to conquer than just Sally's fears. An ancient enemy has followed him, one that threatens all of the Omega Lords, and he discovers that Sally not only holds the key to his heart, but to the very survival of the Clans.

As a relentless foe works to end the Omega for all time, Drake has to convince Sally that she is worthy of love; she in turn must accept what she once thought was impossible. The fates of all the Clans are in their hands. Failure means certain death. With a world in the balance, can one woman find the strength to believe?

CHRISTMAS WITH THE DRAGONS

It's Christmastime. Sally's first with her new family, and she's determined to do it right. She wants to introduce the Omega to her favorite holiday. Enemies lurk, Mach and Turbo are fighting, her powers are growing out of anyone's control, and the guys seem determined to be obtuse about it ... but nothing gets between a dragonswan and what she wants, especially not a pregnant one.

Enjoy this glimpse into the world of the Omega and the continuing evolution of the dragon queen.

What People Are Saying About The Omega Chronicles

"I read the story in one sitting because I just couldn't put it down."

— Nita Banks, BookChick Blog Reviews

"A good choice ... I highly recommend."

— LiaL from The Romance Reviews, Four Stars

"The *Last Dragon* was just awesome! The author's storytelling had me hooked from the start. You have to read the entire book to understand all her twist and turns. The Last Dragon deserves 4.5 stars. I look forward to reading more of her books. You'll just have to read the novel to find out what happens next, and the HEA. I highly recommend this author. I will buy books from her in the future."

— DebA from Night Owl Reviews, TOP PICK AWARD

"Great read! This is a great read for anyone who likes paranormal romances that have a diverse group of characters. I have always enjoyed the shifter stories that had different groups having to work together to achieve success. I look forward to reading more stories about all of the shifters. The author has created a story line ripe with opportunities for each of them to help solve a piece of the riddle and help get back home. I am sure each will involve a special woman, too."

— Reviewed by LiaL for TheRomanceReviews.com Amazon Top 100 Reviewer

"I love series like the Black Dagger Brotherhood and Lords of the Underworld and felt that this story just might be something similar. And, I have to confess that I'm glad I took a chance. The story had moments of sweetness and serious moments of intensity toward the end that will absolutely keep you "IN" the story. I definitely look forward to seeing what happens next as Milchon set the stage for the next Omega to find his love and salvation."

— BookChick Blog Reviews

"Dragons, water beings, shadow movers plus their enemies all blend together to make this a really great book. I would have thought this book was good just because it had dragons in it, but once I started reading it I couldn't put it down, and the best thing is it's book one of a series. All the characters have their own special personalities and abilities and despite the fact it's a fantasy, they seem so real! Hot love scenes combine with humor, understanding and the need to keep sane, all these combine to make an outstanding book which has punch, intrigue and love."

— Long and Short Reviews, given a gold star and labeled BEST BOOK

For Book Chick
and book bloggers everywhere,

Thank You.

For the dragon it shall salvation be,
Happiness is found in three.
Clearest sight is found below,
What was gone, must start to show.
Your armor will have to break,
The last will cause the big mistake.
Lay down your inherited power,
Do not stop in the final hour.
Your lives will grow again here,
When the Jewels provide the key to fear.
For the one who is my very own,
Your greatest destiny is alone.

Omegicon Glossary

Catsu — an Omegicon creature, commonly found in the Speed Clan mythology.

Dioscuri — Omegicon version of angels, or helpers to the Great Oracle.

D'jinas — Ancestral land for the mage.

Dragonswan — A female dragon.

Hidden land — Ancestral seat for the air clan.

Kaji — Dragon self.

Kanji — (also known as dragon's breath) A stream of fire that is exhaled in high stress, battle or any other violent confrontation.

Limbolands — Place between Omega and Earth where the dragons retreated to be in stasis while they waited for the world to rise once more.

Nachash — Dragon clan ancestral lands, referred to as The Nachash when speaking of the palace.

Nej — No or negative.

Peleos — The weather Clan Lords palace and where the elementals and gem warrior were created.

Heios — the air clan's castle located high in the mountains

Vale — Warrior clan lands

Ellium — Warrior clan lord ancestral seat

Tian — Light clan's lands

Crystal Palace — Home of the Oracle and the light clan's elite

Esbo — Ancestral land for the ancient gem warriors, long lost from Omega

Mesqa — Speed clan lands

Denphan — Speed clan lord palace

Sanderk — Ancestral seat for the scouts.

Tian — Elemental clan's home, Clan Lords of the weather elementals were lost before the gem warriors

Tindardesh — Water clan main palace.

Tindaridai — Water clan ancestral lands.

Transpotheosis — The shift a paranormal makes from human form to their other self.

Yej — Yes or positive response.

1

M.J. froze on the stairs to the apartment as the noise from the garage bay below reached her. Clanging. Mild cursing. With the heavy scent of oil in the air. Crap. Squirt was at it again. She hoped that whatever was wrong with the car that was in multiple pieces was easy to resolve. Though she was all for Squirt and her projects, well, to be perfectly honest, they were more like obsessions, but she wished they would hit with better timing. This was not the day for Squirt to go missing-into-engineering.

There was work to be done, but there was always more work to be done.

A wave of cloying cologne heralded the arrival of Razor Arlon. Their boss. Her list of things to do that she'd neglected over the last two days flashed through her mind. A crack of thunder split the air. She hoped the windows were closed. But … why would they be? Nothing else was ready for this weekend. They were toast. Dressed in his usual denim shirt with bolo tie, dirty jeans and ancient cowboy hat, Razor looked like a rodeo star who'd seen the wrong end of a bull, over and over again. M.J. knew he had been a driver for a few seconds, and then won the track in a lucky bet, but somehow his complete lack of accomplishment seemed to escape him. The track was in a sheltered area of the valley and was known to open to events earlier in the season than anyone else. Only the most nefarious and risky teams would dare to come here.

M.J. kept trying to tell their boss he could do something real with the place, but he refused to listen. Razor thought he was famous and always right. It was the rest of the world that was wrong, so he had no problem doing everything he could to prove it. "Hey Razor," she greeted him. "I was just going to get on setting up the snack bar for the races this weekend."

"The driver quarters need some work as well."

M.J. shuddered. The bunkhouse, as she liked to call it, was probably the worst building to work on in the entire track. The drivers trashed it, almost certainly in revenge for not being put up in hotels like most tracks insisted. The only way Razor got any kind of events to this ramshackle, decaying facility was these little "perks" he offered the team owners, which the drivers did not appreciate.

It took a while to make it clear to him that she was never going to be one of the benefits he could put on the menu.

She sighed. Living inside the race track was never easy, but it had been the best solution for their needs. When Squirt's Mom died, they had to find new digs fast. The medical bills took everything, and the landlord wanted his greedy disgusting paws on M.J. Possibly Squirt, too, but M.J. got them out before Squirt even knew. Razor was an old friend of Squirt's mom, and this place needed a support staff. The apartment over the garage was almost spacious and the extras were perfect. Squirt had the garage to play in. It did involve long hours at almost no pay, but there were the free living quarters for them, and, after some passionate pleading, she'd managed to get the owner to throw in the back shed for her personal studio.

"M.J.," he bellowed. When she blinked back to the situation, he grunted. "The bunkhouse?"

"Sure. I'm on it."

"I've got that new hotshot Bobby Evers coming in; it better be great."

"How'd you get Bobby to come here?"

"Your little Squirt in there was showing him some new invention. While he was tinkering around, I got him to agree to move in."

"Super." M.J. tried not to show how annoyed she was at the extra work.

"We're taking him and the rest of the early arrivals to the roadhouse tonight. So you'll have some time to get it done. The snack bar needs to be cleaned top-to-bottom, and the food needs to be prepped before the catering crew gets here."

"It'll get done, Razor."

"See to it. Yous two let me down again, I'll kick yous out on your pretty little ass."

"Don't talk about my ass," she snapped. Then, seeing the angry glint in his eyes, she smiled to soften her tone. She tried, even if she failed miserably. "Razor, we'll get it done. You shouldn't worry so much, it'll give you wrinkles."

The aging former team owner scowled at her joke. His bald head was a sea of skin that melted into folds as it turned into his face. He really was a human Shar Pei. "Watch it, girlie."

"Just kidding, Razor."

"Might be better if yous stopped with the jokes, and started with the cleaning. I took the twos of yous in, out of the goodness of my heart—"

"We're cheap and we work hard. You gave us a job, you didn't adopt—"

"Listen up girlie, yous and that sister of yours better start getting shit done or I will kick yous out without a second thought. I know you're doing the work for both of yous. And I don't give a shit. Get everything cleaned up and ready or pack your crap and get the hell out of my park."

M.J. took a deep breath before she tried to answer. "Got it. I'll get it done."

"Damn right yous will," Razor went banging out of the garage without another word.

They had to get out of here. If she had to listen to one more lecture from Razor and his mangling of the word "you," she'd have to strangle him. They needed money though, a lot of it, to continue doing what they loved and actually keep a roof over their heads. Seeing Squirt still hadn't bothered to come out from underneath the car she was working on, M.J. rolled up her sleeves and decided to tackle the driver's house first. It would take the longest. Hopefully Squirt would emerge sometime and pitch in before she hit the snack bar. Please let Squirt come out.

Maybe the physical activity would free her mind to help her find a solution or escape from the constant Razor's edge they were living on, before someone ended up cut and bleeding from his wrinkled face, all over her clean floor.

2

"What the hell is wrong with you?" Mach's roar was easy to hear throughout Sanctuary. Luke froze in the hallway right outside the living room as he let the pain travel through him. It was easier that way. *Don't fight it. Don't tense up.* His entire body pulsed with each agonizing wave. He let the wall hold him steady for a few minutes as he waited for the strength to find out what was wrong now. He felt so cursedly weak. Lately the migraines were hitting faster and lasting much longer. They all had been so hopeful when Sally had come to live with them.

But whatever miracle she represented to the others seemed to have skipped him entirely.

Rounding the corner and entering the living room, even his limited vision allowed him to see the youngest and most fiercely bonded of them standing head-to-head with murder in their eyes. He breathed a sigh of relief when Blade and Stealth came running into the room and moved immediately to separate them. "There's no fighting here," Blade reminded the speed clan.

"It wouldn't be fighting," Turbo said. "It's called putting him out of our misery."

Stealth dragged Mach back when he lunged for his cousin's throat. "You break the Compact, you condemn us all."

"Bullshit," Turbo swore. "The compact only covers our harming the locals."

"Enough." Luke's softly worded command brought reluctant response from the cousins. "You were given an order. Find other women like our

Sally. What of your progress?"

Mach had the grace to look down. "We don't know what to do."

"Turbo," Luke decided the angrier was the one that needed to get out of the house more, "go to the bar where you found our Sally and see if you identify anyone else. Mach, go to Aquos and Stealth, they have all those human toys, so see if the three of you can come up with a plan. The humans enjoy this social media thing. Perhaps that would be helpful." When no one moved, Luke allowed his own temper to finally get free of his closely held control. "Did I stutter?"

He grunted when they moved apart. Turbo stormed out of the house, the front door slam echoing through his skull, almost sending him to his knees. Stealth and Blade guided Mach away, the most irrepressible of them visibly saddened.

Grateful to be alone, Luke collapsed into the center of the largest leather couch, resting his head on the throw cushion. Chaos. If he hadn't had a headache before, he definitely would have had one after that confrontation. The cousins were inseparable. Why they had taken to constantly trying to kill each other escaped him. He wished he were better at leading them. He wished he understood the cousins enough so he could actually resolve this rift … but he had nothing.

A sound, off in the silence of the house, made his eyes open. *Sally*. She was side-stepping down the side of the hallway, glancing with clear guilt on her face behind her. He realized she had bumped into one of the small ornamental tables in the hall where the elementals like to display the pottery they used to document their history. Craning his neck brought on another wave of the splitting pain, but it was worth it to see Sally had even donned socks to aid in her escape. "What are you doing Sally Eversham?"

She jumped so high he feared she came close to cracking the ceiling plaster. "Luke. You scared me."

"I take it Drake has you on lockdown again?"

"Ugh, he's being completely impossible." She came over to where he was sitting and froze when she was a few steps away. "Another headache?"

"Guilty," he confessed. "Now, what's wrong between you and Drake?"

"He's being ridiculous," she collapsed onto the couch jostling him. He used every fiber of his being to not groan at the movement. "He thinks my being pregnant makes me delicate. It's nuts."

"A bonded dragon with a mate expecting their young, is not nuts. It is a force of nature, one you would be wise not to anger."

"Luke, quit with the 'one-ring-to-rule-them-all' crap. It's me. And you're no elf. Drake doesn't understand. A woman can do anything while pregnant, including spending time with her friends."

"Male friends," he softly amended her.

"It's the only kind I have here," she grumbled. "The female elementals never have any time just to hang out, and they don't really seem to like spending free time."

"The elementals like working," he shrugged. "Free time isn't really a concept with which they have any association. Clearly we have been amiss. I apologize if you hunger for female companionship--"

"I don't," she interrupted him. "You guys are the greatest. It's just ..."

"What?"

Sally sighed so deeply he smiled a little at the longing it displayed. "I've never had a family before who liked spending time with me. When I hang out with you guys, I love it. I need the time we all chill together. It's not physically taxing for me to sit and watch anime with Mach and Turbo. It's actually relaxing to play video games with Stealth and Blade."

"I've seen you do both," Luke chuckled. "I wouldn't call it relaxing."

"Well, it is to me."

"Sally, Drake worships you. Just tell him; he'll give you whatever you need. His dragon nature would not allow any less."

"I have—" she abruptly cut off whatever else she was going to say as a wave of pain once more washed through him taking his vision, reason, even the breath from his body. "Luke," she softened her tone to a bare whisper. "How bad is this one?"

"Worst yet," he gritted out through his clenched teeth.

"Hold on."

Time seemed endless when he was lost in the pain lands. He had no way of marking how long she was gone. There was only one wave of pain after the other. When she returned he could sense it from her light floral scent. It was the greatest irony to him that these attacks brought heightened senses, which only seemed to exacerbate the torture. The only reason his stomach wasn't emptying out was he'd learned to just not eat anything. His dignity was far safer that way. "I'm going to press a cold cloth against your head," she explained. The feeling of the icy fabric seemed to force the pain back a bit, for which he did not have enough words of gratitude. "Now, why don't you lie down, and put your head on my lap. You said my proximity was helpful to ease these attacks. Let me help."

"Drake—"

"My husband will understand and appreciate my desire to assist his friend." Her hands cupped his shoulders and he was guided up and then onto her lap. When his body was fully horizontal, he again felt some of the pain level ease. The fabric was adjusted so it now covered his forehead and his eyes. "I have replacement cloths in a basin next to me," she whispered.

"You'll get bored just sitting and watching me sleep," he protested.

"Nonsense," her hand soothed over his hair and he had to admit, at least to himself, that she was correct about it helping. He didn't know what to call this ... tending. His mother was never one for childhood care, and it was clearly something to be valued. "I'll be fine right here. The television has been on mute since I came back in. You guys have like seven billion channels. I am sure I'll find something absorbing to spend a few hours on."

Luke smiled slightly, "Nothing too girly."

"I will choose a show appropriately manly so if anyone finds us they won't tease you," she promised him.

"You are truly the best of women," he praised. "And the wisest."

"Tell my husband that."

 3

He watched the Range Rover go squealing out of the drive and into the night. This was only getting easier. He was shocked at how lax the Clan Lords had grown over the last few years. Their abandonment of the old ways was leading them to new levels of pain. Just as he always planned it. From the beginning he knew this world would give him the one thing he truly wanted; his clan had planned it for centuries: total annihilation of the Omegicon.

Tossing the vial in the air, he easily caught it as it tumbled. It had taken him years to brew the formula within.

Reaching the outer walls of Sanctuary, he followed the left wing until he found the hatch he was looking for. The well head. Perfect. Opening it up, he uncorked his little surprise for the Clan Lords and poured it into the water below. This was the final dose he'd prepared. He'd been smart. Using it slowly. Eroding their strength, chipping away at their bodies' natural resistance. Closing the cover, he tried to resist the lure of gloating. His plan was working.

A sound, a noise off from the peace of the country night, made him whirl around in surprise

Crouching down, he gathered the shadows around him as his eyes continued to pierce the darkness. The ability to cloak in the darkness was not meant to be his kind's ability, but he'd stolen it from the others years ago. Again, he heard a sound, the crack of a twig breaking under the step of a boot somewhere in the distance. *Where was it? Who was it?*

An owl suddenly took off from the tree to his left.

Howling mad, a feral cat darted out from the brush and went chasing after an evening meal.

Was it innocent? Just the normal sounds of nature jarring him from his moment of ego? Perhaps he was wrong?

The last time he'd allowed his sense of self importance to take prevalence was when he'd been given his new name. The architect. He didn't remember when the elementals had started to call him that. He thought it might have been because he was so different from the others, they felt compelled to set him apart. His work was always meant to take eons. There was no way to speed through these plans. Even when he saw an opportunity, the taking of Blade and using him to eradicate a group of the Clan Lords at once, things had gone wrong. He had never foreseen the dragon finding a mate, or how powerful she might be. He returned to the original plan, leaving behind all distractions.

Now any disturbance of his plans could make his entire house come down.

When he could not detect any further noise he decided it must have been the cat. Wild animals. He detested such chaos.

Moving swiftly to the cover of the trees, avoiding the Scout camps, he paused when he made it into the tree line. Shoe prints. It had been a spy, after all. Kneeling next to the sign that someone witnessed his activity, his hand tightened on the hilt of his sword. Someone knew.

* * *

Blade kept his hand on Mach's shoulder as they moved through Sanctuary. A quick glance from Stealth was all it took to redirect their progress to his room. He'd just set up a new area in his suite and he guessed it might be the perfect distraction for their youngest brother. "I just don't understand."

Cringing at Mach's muttered confession, Blade tried to console him. "Turbo's changed, Mach. We all see it."

"I don't understand what's going on."

Blade shook his head at Mach's whisper. "His anger is going to get him hurt."

"The only one hurting seems to be me."

Stealth was glad they'd reached the entrance to his room. "Maybe this will help get your mind off things."

Opening the door, he gave Mach a little push to step inside. "I still don't get why he's so pissed off. We always joke—" Mach's sentence cut off when he looked around the room for the first time, his eyes bulging. "Holy Oracle, Stealth … Blade … what did you guys do?"

"Stealth and Aquos have been working on this for months."

Blade's explanation did little to lessen Mach's wonder. "The technology isn't this advanced." Mach ran his fingers over the bank of flat screens angled around the raised platform. "How did you do this?"

"Humans have the pieces. All we did was put them together in a different configuration. It helps that we have as much money as we do. We were able to purchase the pieces from multiple vendors and re-purpose them into what we need. Blade's been our test subject."

"Brother ... this is amazing. How's it work?"

Stealth started pressing buttons. "Blade's been helping with the configurations for the training program, but we've been waiting for you to test it out."

"Really?"

"Of course, brother." Blade's elbow bumped Mach. The virtual reality program was soon running and he handed the youngest member of the Speed clan the headsets. "Put these on and step onto the platform." As soon as he did, Mach was elevated several inches off the magnetic surface. "It took us a while to get the suspension to work, but I think now that it does you can really get the virtual reality aspect of the experience."

"It's just like I dreamed."

Five words. Mach's five words said an endless amount to Blade and Stealth, making the months of work worth it. They shared a smile as Mach began to experience the one thing they hadn't been able to access for thousands of years. Home.

 4

Drake ran through the halls, his faith in his woman the only thing that kept his wings from exploding out of his skin. *Where was she? Maybe she went for a snack?* Being pregnant with his young had made Sally finally embrace her passionate nature, especially where food was concerned. *Yes. Food.* Food is an acceptable reason to sneak out of his bed. Of course, she knows the elementals would provide whatever she needed if she asked, but his woman seemed to enjoy cooking, and he liked his woman happy. So she must have made love to him all night long, another benefit to her embracing her passionate side, and then gotten hungry.

This was acceptable.

Which was when he saw her cuddling with Luke on the couch.

If he could have torn his eyes away from his woman he'd have noticed Blade and Stealth wandering in.

"Honey—"

"No, honey," Drake yelled.

"Keep your voice down," she whispered gesturing at the sleeping Luke whose head was on her lap. "You knew I didn't go far. Luke's in pain. He has a horrible headache."

"I'm up now," Luke slowly sat, his eyes warily trained on Drake. "She was just trying to heal me, dragon."

Sally stood up, "Drake. What's wrong?"

"Mate, I have told you over and over," Drake took a deep breath. His intention was to speak calmly, it really was. Instead his next words came out in a complete roar. "You do not sneak out of my bed."

"It's our bed," Sally put her hands on her hips.

"Whatever," he snarled.

"Dude," Mach came sauntering in, "try chilling."

"My kind does not chill," he roared again.

"I humbly apologize for distracting your mate with my need," Luke gave Drake a deep bow. "I fear her kindness has angered you unnecessarily."

Sally took several steps toward her husband. "No, Luke. You don't need to apologize." She reached Drake and immediately punched him in the solar plexus. He gave a slight grunt to appease her. The transformation since she'd discovered her dragon side had made her stronger, but he'd had eons to develop his hide. Her blow felt like a tickle. Realizing his woman was still yelling, he tried to focus on her words and resist the urge to throw her over his shoulder and fly her back to the limbo lands. "—And don't you even try to tell me what I can and cannot do in my own home. Luke offered his protection when you sent me back to my homicidal family. You don't get to argue when I'm trying to help him or any of the other guys."

Focusing on her again, Drake's eyebrows rose when he realized how high Sally's temperature had gotten in the last few breaths. Watching her face color a bright red, he knew what was about to happen. The guilt he felt that he had not warned her was a sorrow to share with her another day. "Sally-mine ..."

"I like the guys and I matter to them. How can you even try to keep me from going to them when they need me? Selfish is never sexy."

"Sally-mine, calm down." He held up his hands to her, wishing he could prevent what he saw was about to happen. His world was so new to her, he'd never considered how much she still had to learn. There never seemed to be enough time. Subtly he moved so she would be facing the right direction, shooting warning glances at his friends so they were safely out of range.

"Calm down," she punched his chest again. "Calm down," her voice escalated to an eardrum splitting level. "How could you tell me to calm down," the last was said so loud he was sure she shattered glass.

"Because you need to?"

Mach's question was the proverbial straw for the camel's back. When she whirled on him, her face grew neon red. "Down," Drake bellowed at everyone and dove for his woman. He managed to turn her back toward the fireplace before the stream of fire erupted from her mouth. Holding her tightly to his chest, he waited until she was done. He knew this process only too well. She couldn't be moved until the kanji was depleted. There was no fighting when the dragon's breath had control. It was why he insisted on having all of the fireplaces when they originally built Sanctuary. He had these for emergencies when he lost control, and he'd had centuries to perfect it. Sally had only discovered her dragon side in the last few months.

"Dude," Mach's drawl distracted him for a moment from his shuddering woman. "That. Was. Awesome."

On one hand he wished to agree with his young friend. On the other, he wanted to punch him in the jaw. It wasn't like Mach ever felt that when Drake was going through his kanji attacks.

"What was that?"

He turned and cradled Sally. The blaze in the fireplace made a cheery light as he tried to break this depressing news. "Kanji," he smoothed her strawberry curls from her damp forehead. "Dragon's breath. Sweetheart, I'm so sorry I didn't warn you this could happen."

"Not your fault," Sally patted his hand on her side.

"So she's like really a dragon now? Awesome," Mach went to high-five Stealth who gave him a confused look and turned away. Mach's shoulders slumped, "I miss T."

"It is my young who forces this change on you," Drake felt compelled to point out to her.

"This is our baby," she squeezed his hand. When she started to sit up, he immediately moved to help her. "I'm okay, Drake."

"Kanji is physically and mentally exhausting."

"As is carrying a baby," Sally rose to her feet, Drake's arms around her, concerned she might collapse. "I'm fine."

Stealth, Blade and Mach took a few steps closer to them. Drake was surprised at the distance Luke seemed to want to keep between him and the others. "Someone needs to tell the elementals to keep the fireplaces stocked."

Just then, a gold and a red elemental came in with their arms filled with wood. Blade smiled, "Drake … did you really think they wouldn't know?"

The elementals filled the basket next to the stone hearth, bowed to them, and withdrew.

"Sally, I am so sorry." Drake knelt before his mate and laid his head in her lap.

"Drake, Tamar warned me this would happen. He said the baby would speed the transformation when I accepted the throne." She brushed his hair from his face and smiled when he opened his eyes to look at her. "It's ok, honey."

"You need rest," he growled. Smoothly rising, he wrapped her in his arms, released his wings and flew them back to their nest.

5

Turbo entered the club, still fuming over the fight between him and Mach. If he was being honest, however, he was angry all the time lately. Letting the pulsing rhythms of the music pounding through the club travel through him, he took a deep breath in. Same old, same old. Stale beer, piss, cloying female scent of women determined to find a hook-up, and churning levels of desperation. Nothing. No scent of home. No tickling at the back of his nose as memories of their planet streamed through the air. Seeing his favorite booth was taken, he stomped over to the only available table. It was right outside the back room, but at least people were separate from it. He turned the wood chair around, and rested his arms on the seat back. Motioning to his favorite waitress from across the room he nodded with approval when he saw her immediately grab a bottle of Jack and hustle over.

Watching the crowd of moving couples, he tried to scope someone he wanted. There were twins by the bar, long blonde hair, bright pink lips, nails were even done. Just the kind he liked.

Thinking about all the times he would have challenged Mach to see how many honeys they could rack up in a single night, he scowled at the duo trying to look at him coyly through their fake eyelashes and the fall of their hair.

No. No way.

He wished he could stop hating everyone. He wished he could stop feeling so mad at everything he saw. He wished he could stop knowing he wasn't meant to be alive.

Unfortunately, if wishes were horses he might actually beat Mach in a drag race for a change.

A round of boisterous laughter came from the back room. Turning, he was shocked to see a girl come running out of the greasy curtain. The brief glimpse he got of her was a female in an ancient and equally hideous granny dress, with some kind of dust all over her clothes, teetering on a pair of heels like a newborn colt. Then it hit him. Home. Pure and clean as if he just stepped foot on the shore outside his ancestral seat, the breeze coming in clear across the waves.

Jumping up from the chair, he sidestepped the waitress with the bottle and tray, following the smell, he made it outside to see his prey take a header on the other side of the packed parking lot.

Perfect.

Coming up behind her he froze when he heard her softly weeping. A wave of rage flooded him and he wanted to return to that back room and tear every motherfucker apart with his bare hands.

"Stupid, stupid, stupid," she whispered. "Why would you even try?"

Turbo watched as she curled into the fetal position, her body still rocking with her deep, racking sobs. *He didn't have time for this.* He had no idea how to handle an emotional female. This was not his area. Wishing Mach was here so he could just get the car, and Mach could calm the woman, he shrugged. Reaching down, he slid his hand into the crook of her neck, and squeezed hard. Pop. Leaking girly turned instantly to silent dead weight. That will work. Hefting her up from the ground, he almost threw her. She was a lot lighter than she looked. No curves on this one. She was all straight away. Pity. He tended to like his partners built with plenty of turns.

Getting to the Range Rover he wondered how long the nerve pinch thing would work. Concerned she'd wake up in the middle of the drive home, Turbo changed direction to the back hatch.

He'd installed a wild animal cage a while ago, just in case. The reinforced dog cage was perfect for any emergencies his new issues might cause. She might as well ride inside where she couldn't hurt either of them.

Behind the wheel he finally felt some peace. *Girl secured.* At least when he got home he could shut Luke up and hopefully the female would distract everyone from getting all up in his shit. He just wanted to be left alone. They'd achieved peace in Sanctuary for the first time ever, and he almost wished they could go back to their former bristling animosity when they could go weeks without seeing each other. Turbo wondered how this female fit into the prophecy.

Who did she belong to?

Sally and Drake were such an instant natural fit … no matter how much Aquos wished otherwise. *Who would this girl heal?*

Turbo put his money on Luke.

He'd been so sick lately. No matter how much he tried to hide it, even Turbo in his perpetual rage had noticed.

Last person he'd let near her was Mach. Bastard didn't deserve it.

It would suck if the woman he found, ended up binding to the one guy he actually wanted to kill.

* * *

Moving lightly on her feet, Avaris traveled from shadow-to-shadow, her eyes seeking out any sign of activity in the darkness. The robed guy with the vial had shocked her. She'd never heard his approach. If it wasn't for her connection to wild things, she knew he would have combed through the area until he uncovered her hiding place. *What the hell is that guy doing with the well?* Shaking off her musing, she opened the center door into the house.

There was no time to be concerned about the odd events surrounding this place.

She had responsibilities. Ones that could not wait any longer.

Inside the giant kitchen she froze when she heard a noise in the distance. The servants should all be asleep. She'd watched the house for two days before making this foray. The truth was, she'd continue to monitor their movements, hoping for confirmation of the schedule if they hadn't finally run out of food.

Her girls needed food or they'd get cranky.

And her girls being cranky was never a good thing.

Survive. Keep them alive. This was the only rule she'd been given when she woke in this world.

And the hardest one to accomplish.

When the blond man had let her in here, given her sanctuary, she'd been on the run from something for days. Seeing this place, all the open territory, it was a dream come true. The girls were happy here. They weren't peaceful, but her girls never were. At least here she could let them be who they were without concern of witnesses. The only thing they were missing was food. Going to the far side of the kitchen, she opened the door she'd found the last time she was inside. Running from the attack on the building, feeling almost overwhelming guilt over her abandonment of her responsibilities. Slipping into the small storehouse, she used her glow stick to light what she'd found. Food. Shelves and shelves of it. Opening her backpack, Avaris worked fast to load it up. This was good. Even better than good.

Survive. Keep them alive. She finally had a chance to do both.

 6

The echoing bang of the front door broke the guys from their stupor. Turbo stood in the entryway staring at the other Clan Lords. Brothers. Best friends. *Why did he hate them? How could he?* Pushing aside his enmity for them, he tried to take a deep breath to bury his emotion. His heart might be screaming one thing, but his brain told him not to listen. For once, he was determined to obey his brain. If he had to be the last of his kind, he'd like to be the smartest as well.

"Dude, you would not believe what you just missed."

Mach's words made him scowl. He'd missed this event Mach wanted to repeat to him because he'd been kicked out of the house. Didn't he remember that? *Fucker.* "Come," he barked to them all.

Outside he waited by the back of the car, his hand tapping against his leg. He wanted to retreat to the woods and let the solitude soothe his jagged edges. Lately it was only there he would find any peace. But first, he needed to pass off this burden he found on someone more equipped to handle it. He may not have much control right now, but it became quickly evident he was sadly out of his depth where this surprise package was concerned.

"What is amiss?"

Turbo ignored Blade's question. He was momentarily struck by the incongruousness of how the others were standing. Mach, Stealth and Blade were a few paces away. Luke was keeping a foot away from the rest. What's up with that? When did the Son of Light decide he was better than everyone else?

"I brought you a gift," he announced. Opening the gate, he turned back to his friends when he heard movement inside. Good. It was still alive. "I wish to be clear. I tried Mach's way."

"The nerve pinch?"

He nodded to Mach's question. "I tried it. Three times. It didn't work. She kept waking up."

Luke put his hand over his face and groaned. "What did you do?"

"I clocked her."

"You punched a woman?" Stealth yelled so loud it must have reached through the stone walls of Sanctuary because Aquos came running out.

"You did what?"

"I punched a woman ... gently," he swore to Aquos, who was shimmering with rage. Seeing his assurances were doing little to calm anyone, and the noises inside the vehicle were growing louder, he gave up on the telling and chose to go for the showing. "Here." Lifting the hatch, they could all see the interior. The cage he had installed a few weeks before was his little secret, but he guessed everyone knew about it now. He'd locked the female inside of it for both their safety. The girl looking out at them though, appeared nothing but harmless. Her big eyes were staring at them with stark accusation, and he felt a surge of guilt at the bruise his improved eyesight could discern in the glow of the ceiling light. The dust he noticed when he'd first seen her was still everywhere, her skin and clothes were covered with it. When Blade reached in to release the gate, he pushed him back "Careful. She's a hell of a fighter, and has a mean left hook."

"Get back. All of you," Aquos bellowed, shoving Blade and Turbo away from the hatch.

"Dude, chill," Mach suggested. "You haven't even met the girl."

 7

M.J. kept pressing back into the wire mesh of the cage, trying to see a way out. That's what she did best. Escape. But this time, she couldn't see any possible path to freedom. She never even heard the monster who'd found her in the parking lot. Crying her eyes out over those guys. Going to that ridiculous club to try and talk the drivers into endorsing Squirt's engine had seemed like a good idea. Dressing sexy was her only way of getting past the bouncers and into the back room where the party was being held. Unfortunately, she didn't have those types of clothes, so she raided Squirt's Mom's trunk. The clothes were thirty years out of style and made for a woman who embodied only those traits that were soft and girly.

Which was everything M.J. was not.

She knew the first mistake she made was when she stopped in her studio for courage. Looking at her beautiful sculptures always made her feel stronger somehow. More able to face these types of situations. Of course, once she started looking, she was led to polishing, which left her with dust covering her from head to toe.

Now she wished she was covered with armor instead.

"I'm Aquos," the nice one explained. The other towering men were all sent backwards from his scathing glare. *This one was different somehow.* She figured the funky lighting was screwing with his skin color, which was actually blue. Otherwise, he looked like a swimmer or a fencer, with wide shoulders, long arms and a narrow waist. He was taller than the joking one and the monster who'd taken her and then punched her when she wouldn't stop screaming, but the same height as the others. His cropped dark hair and stubbled chin made him fit for a magazine cover. The haunted look in his eyes and lines of pain radiating out from their corners called to her heart. "I apologize for Turbo. He's a complete ass. If you want me to hold him down so you can beat him up, I will. It'd be my pleasure."

"Try it, waterboy," Turbo snarled.

"Excellent choice, dude." The joking one went to high five Turbo, who just turned away in disgust. "I really miss, T."

"He's heading for the woods," one of the others pointed out unnecessarily.

"Bite me."

"Shut it," Aquos snarled at them. Turning again to her, he held out his hand. "I swear to the Oracle, no one will hurt you."

"The one who left hurt me."

"He will not have a second chance," the nice one swore.

"I'm Luke," the one farthest away introduced himself. "That's Mach, Stealth and Blade. Turbo is the one who left. You have my deepest apologies for him. I swear you have nothing to fear from us."

"Never said I was afraid."

"There is no shame if you are," Aquos gave her a small smile.

M.J. lifted her chin as she continued to press against the rear of the cage, "I'm not."

"I apologize for the way you were brought here,'" Luke said again.

"He kidnapped me." M.J. caught the flinch of pain that flashed on the one called Aquos' face. He staggered slightly, caught himself on the side of the car, and straightened. "Are you ok?"

She guessed her whispered question was just heard by him, for only he smiled. "Please don't be scared."

"It's hard not to be." If they wanted to think she was scared, let them. Usually, it made it easier to escape when people underestimated you.

"Luke wouldn't lie to you, he's allergic to falsehoods. I swear you are safe here."

M.J. bit her lip as she tried to figure out what to do. Sure, the cage was a trap but at least it's something she'd gained an understanding of over the last hour. Looking up, her tension eased when the stranger with the blue skin gave her a warm smile. Everything in her responded to this man. It was as if she'd been searching for something all of her life and had found it in this one person's eyes.

It scared the hell out of her.

"Please," she slid into the light a little, so he could see her. "Just let me go home."

Aquos shook his head. "That is the last thing I can do."

"Why?" M.J. moved closer. Let him see what she looked like. Understand she was no girly-girl, no damsel in distress. This was the type of guy who deserved some shiny armor and an appropriate fainting woman in his arms.

She was not the fainty type.

In truth, she was more likely the one who cleaned up for the fainty type.

Luke started to join them, and instead took several steps away. "Miss … our friend brought you here because we are in desperate need of women—"

M.J. dove for the back of the cage.

"Don't do that," Aquos started to reach for her, but instead turned on Luke. "Shut it, Light-boy. You're scaring her."

"I thought if she understood how much we need her …"

"So what? All of you are planning on raping me?"

"No," they all yelled in unison. Well. O.k. *That was either comforting or vastly insulting.*

Aquos took a deep breath. "We just want a chance to get to know you."

"Why not try going to a bar like your serial killer friend?"

Aquos gestured to his skin and hair. "For obvious reasons."

"You let the goth thing go a little far, but it's nothing I haven't seen before."

"Really?" The hot one seemed to perk up at her comment and glanced at his friends. "Why didn't you guys tell me that?"

They all looked confused at the question.

Luke shrugged. "You've changed so much over the last few weeks. We all have since Sally joined us."

"There's another woman here?" she asked with hope.

"Yes," Aquos promised.

"And on any other day we would have let her handle this," Blade explained.

"She's currently incapacitated."

"What'd you do to her?"

All of the men flinched at her question. "Where is Sally?" Aquos seemed just as confused as she felt, so she moved closer to him.

"Sally's experienced her first kanji."

"No shit …" Aquos drawled. The pride in his face made M.J. want to find this Sally and hurt her.

Which made no freaking sense.

"Look," she put on her best let's-be-reasonable tone, the one she only employed when Squirt was being especially a pain in the ass. "How about you all go check on this Sally, since you seem to be so worried about her, and I'll just take myself home. If one of you lends me a cell phone, I'll call a cab."

"No cab companies," Aquos snapped.

"Fine," she rolled her eyes. "An Uber."

"None of those either," he said.

"I think they've got this under control," Stealth and Blade turned to leave. When Mach continued to stand and watch, Blade grabbed him by the neck and dragged him with them.

"Come on," he complained. "It was just getting good."

When it was only the three of them, Aquos reached his hand to her. "I swear by all that is holy and good. I vow on my very life, if you wish. No harm will come to you in this place."

Luke gave him a look of shock.

"He hit me." M.J. remembered waking up in the back of an unknown SUV, locked in a cage and screaming. She thought she'd make a break for it when the driver she couldn't see pulled over. Instead all she saw was a gigantic fist aimed right for her jaw. He did this several times. "Hard."

"I know," Aquos sighed. "For that crime I shall make him pay."

This time when he reached his hand to her, she took it. His fingers were colder than ice as they wrapped around hers. She repressed the shiver they caused, and locked her muscles harder when another kind of shimmer traveled through her. "Why do I trust you?"

"Your soul ..."

"My soul?"

"Your soul recognizes its own."

His dark eyes blazed and she let his grip guide her to the edge of the cage this time. "I think you're all nuts," she muttered.

"No," he gave her another of those melty smiles, "you don't."

Pausing at the edge of the trunk she swung her legs out to hang down. Her shoes were gone, the ruffled, flowered skirt dirty and torn. Well, she didn't look good in any of this anyway, and it wasn't like Squirt cared about these clothes. Only thing Squirt cared about was things that went fast. "So what's the plan, boys? If you intend to keep me here, I'd appreciate not being locked up. I'm not a big fan of tight spaces."

"I share this dislike," Aquos confessed.

"We all do," Luke added.

"So I stay here to see if you guys what ... like me? Let me share a little secret. Guys don't generally see me as anything other than another human."

"Well," Aquos smiled. "Let me share a secret with you. We're not human."

"Funny."

Aquos gave her his hand to help her down from the Rover's gate, and for once, M.J. decided to take it. When she jumped down however it was Aquos who needed her support. A wave of pain seemed to hit him, almost crumpling him to the floor.

M.J. caught him before he hit. At first she tried to keep him standing, but he was a great deal heavier than he looked. When she realized she

22

couldn't keep him upright, she tried for the trunk, and instead his sheer overwhelming weight bore both of them straight to the ground.

Which was when she realized his friend hadn't done anything to help. "Excuse you?"

"I'm sorry," Luke paled, but stayed frozen in his spot.

"Help him," she ordered the blond angelic-looking guy who continued to stand still and stare at her.

"I … I …I …"

"At least call the others," she begged him. "I can't lift him by myself."

"They won't come. They can't take the chance."

"For what?" M.J. guided Aquos's head to her lap and tried to feel for a pulse in his neck. When she felt no beat, she moved her hand to the center of his chest. A comforting thump was evident beneath her palm, though it felt unnaturally fast. "Isn't he your friend?"

"We suffer from a disease," Luke crouched next to them. "You can't catch it, but we definitely are the ones in danger. They'd be afraid he's contagious."

"What kind of disease can you catch that I can't?"

"One that's killing us." She gazed at him, stunned. Her eyes blinked a few times while she tried to process his words. Luke's eyebrow rose with surprise, "You aren't scared?"

"Not of him," M.J. took Aquos's hand in hers and squeezed. He was still so cold. "Can you help me get him to a hospital?"

"They won't be able to save him."

"So who will?"

"We have a place he uses when he's sick." The look he gave her was filled with concern. "This will put you square in the middle of our world. Are you sure you're ready for this?"

She looked up at the towering stone mansion where they were parked, the dog cage that had brought her here, down to the unconscious gorgeous man lying in her lap. It was a scene straight out of the fairy tales she read as a child, and many of the romance books she consumed like an addict as an adult. "Seems to me that option was decided when the monster clocked me."

"Yes," Luke winced. "We will all pay for that one."

"Good. Now, help me get him someplace more comfortable, please."

 8

M.J. could barely take in the grandeur of the mansion as they shuffled through the many halls. She appreciated the assistance from the guy with the floppy blond hair, but the one who looked like he could run the special forces and the green berets may have been more help. She was stuck holding most of the unconscious Aquos up, with the Luke-guy navigating. The dead weight that was the block of ice she was calling her new friend was scaring her.

And after years in foster care, not much scared her. Ever. *Except Squirt, in a let's-invent-something fever.*

When they reached their destination, she almost stopped them in their tracks, which would have sent her patient tumbling to the ground. Blond guy groaned when he grabbed her patient to steady him. "This is where he lives?"

"It's the place we made for when he's sick," Luke said.

M.J. decided to keep her mouth shut. Inside she was saddened. These men have so much, there was no hint of financial difficulty anywhere in this house. So why the hell was the nicest one of them stuck in what was little more than a hovel? The room they were in was nothing but a giant empty pool, with a single raft in the middle. A virtual sea of white ceramic subway tile barely broken by the golden tones of the wood door. Her assistant settled Aquos into the raft. *This isn't normal. It's not even safe.* The drain at the far end of the pool wasn't even covered. She couldn't keep her derision inside. "I thought you guys were friends."

He looked at her with surprise. "We are. We consider him a brother."

"Well, with family like you, who the hell needs enemies?"

Luke shrugged. "He's never complained."

"He wouldn't," she snapped. "He's too nice. You might have tried to convince him to accept something better."

"You don't even know him. Is there something else you need?"

She bit her lip to keep from barking at him more. "I guess you did enough."

"Any supplies or food," he gestured to the empty tile chamber.

"What?"

He sighed. "Well, if you change your mind, just get him to say what you need out loud and someone will hear and deliver."

"So there's some kind of high tech intercom system?"

"You could say that."

"I guess I just did."

Blondie shuddered, and the color drained from his face like someone had pulled out his cork. M.J. took several steps closer to him, and brushed his arm. The heat from his skin was so high it felt like it seared her straight through. "You're sick, too. Who's going to take care of you?"

"Mine escaped during the dragon attack."

She watched him leave, her mouth hanging open. Okay. *Guess that fever was even higher than she thought.*

"I don't know your name—" A hacking cough attack made her rush over to the Aquos guy. Crouching next to him she grimaced at the pool walls.

"My name is M.J." She brushed her hand across his face wincing at the iciness of his skin. "You need a blanket."

Before she could wake him to get him to repeat the command a crack on the door made her turn to witness a small robed creature push a cart into the chamber. Going over she found blankets, pillows, drinks, snacks and some candles. Wow. *So the super high-tech intercom system works for her, too?*

Someone should tell Silicon Valley.

"M.J. is a beautiful name."

"Hush it, goth-boy." She rushed back to him with a pillow and blankets in her arms. Spreading the quilt over him, she crouched beside him to help him lean up so she could put the pillow behind his head. "I should warn you. I used to take care of my foster brothers and sisters, but I offer no guarantee at how good I am at the Florence Nightingale thing."

"Who?"

"She was a famous nurse," M.J. explained. *Who doesn't know who Florence Nightingale is?* Maybe they're illegal aliens?

"Never heard of her. Any way you wish to help me I would accept with gladness. I do not deserve your kindness, but I—" Another round of that hacking cough. M.J. held him close to her chest, trying desperately to help him through the fit. She smoothed her hand over his back, wishing she could give him some of her warmth. A shiver rocked her as his lack of heat seemed to drain her of her own. "You should go. There are several guest rooms across the hall. Please pick one."

"I'm not leaving you."

Aquos shook his head. "I can't do this. Turbo's crimes against you haven't been addressed. I cannot take more—"

"Hush it, goth-boy," she repeated. "I don't leave people in need."

"Good," he took a quivering breath. "Then you will never leave me."

"Big talk for a sick goth-boy. How about you get some rest and then we'll discuss how long I'm staying."

"I should—"

"How about you give up thoughts like 'I should' until you feel better," she commanded him. "Now, angel-face ..."

Her voice grew quiet as he got hit by another round of hard coughing while he made an additional noise she'd never heard before. "Angel-face?" he hacked up another lung. "I take it you mean Luke?"

She nodded. He started with the rumbly sound again, which was when she realized he was actually laughing. It made her smile, "Come on. If the shoe fits ..."

"Angel face," he nodded. "The others are going to love that one."

"Well before ... Luke, dragged us into this tile refuge that even a virus wouldn't want to live in, I didn't know there were any other options. You said there are guest rooms across the hall. If they have normal beds, why don't we move this little ICU moment to one of those?"

"Right," Aquos tried to lunge to get up but only managed to fall to the side, necessitating her settling him back on the raft.

"Just tell me what you need," she ordered him while centering him on the pillow.

"I can't. I have to do it myself, the elementals won't respond to you."

"They just did." She pointed to the cart with supplies and the blanket she tucked around him. "See? We're going to be fine."

"It isn't right. Something is bound to happen and I don't want you to get scared."

"Like I said," she adjusted his blankets higher on his shoulders and tried tucking it around him for good measure. "I don't scare easy."

"That's good. Because I'm terrified all the time."

M.J.'s eyes flew to his, but he'd already drifted into sleep. Good. *It will help him heal.* His words. Why did what he said just blow open some door in her heart she hadn't even known she had? Sighing, she brushed her hand over his head. He was still so cold. How do you heat someone up that feels like a block of ice? She never in her life imagined she'd actually long for some global warning. Glancing up, she waited for another cracking knock on the door, but nothing happened.

Guess that telepathic intercom doesn't always work.

"M.J ..."

He was calling for her? Clasping his fingers in her hands, she tried to squeeze some of her strength into him. She was always so healthy. She never got sick. Right now, she'd suffer through a hundred colds in exchange for this man's good health. M. J. Storm. Always so level-headed. Always using her common sense. She never even made a birthday wish.

But for him? For him, she would.

 9

Luke went into the hall and set out to find Turbo. Did he not understand the rules of the Compact protected them as much as it was in place to safeguard the humans? How could he do this? Turbo had been different since the attack that had almost killed him, but he had always been one of the kindest of the Clan Lords. He and Mach had a bond that was untouchable, even when the Omegicon were at their worst. Speed had come to this world with the most clan members still living. They'd lost so much, but never had he seen any kind of deviance like hitting a human female. Women were precious to their kind; they knew too well what a world was like without them. This violence in his friend's actions stunned him. *He hit her.* A human female, and more than once from the look of the bruises on the side of the girl's face. Luke had wanted to puke at the violence visited on the weaker form: violence enacted under his watch.

He was only able to track Turbo down to the woods because he'd left a door open. The oldest surviving member of the Speed Clan was staring out at the trees that nestled Sanctuary in their midst. "How could you?"

"You told me to find women like Sally. She's like Sally."

"I didn't think I'd have to tell you not to abuse them in the process."

Turbo whirled around to face him, and Luke took several steps back. He looked like he was ready to kill, and Luke wondered if he'd have the strength to fight him if he acted. "I did what I had to. She wouldn't stop fighting."

"Which means you show her more kindness, not less." Luke grabbed the tree trunk to keep from falling to the ground. He had to get to his own room soon or even Turbo would realize the truth he was hiding. His illness had gotten so much worse. They were all so hopeful when they'd found Sally. All of them had seen their symptoms disappear for a while, but they were steadily coming back. Aquos was clearly suffering, and now he was too. This madness would destroy them all.

"I did what I had to do," Turbo shrugged.

"T ... this isn't you. Why are you so mad all the time? What the hell is going on?"

"Look at our illustrious leader. What? You want to get all touchy-feely with me now, Luke? I don't swing that way, man. You know better."

"Neither do I," only through his years of discipline could he push the pain he felt at the girl he'd lost during the mercenary attack. "Turbo, talk to me. Let me help. I am your friend."

"I have no friends," Turbo went running into the woods, tearing off his shirt.

Luke looked at the discarded garment on the bush a few yards ahead of him, confused. *What the hell?* Turbo's angry all the time and he's streaking?

Sighing, he realized standing in the woods wasn't going to get him any answers, but asking for some help might.

He could only pray he'd be answered.

10

M.J. kept piling on blankets and trying to ignore the line of carts she was racking up against the wall. They just kept coming with stuff. No people. No physicians. Not even a physician manual. "This isn't helping. I could really use some guidance," she yelled out to the closed door.

No answer.

"I don't know what I'm doing."

Aquos lunged to the side and caught M.J.'s hand in his. "I would gladly walk through hell with you, my M.J. I trust your I-don't-know-what-I'm-doing far more than any expert this cruel world provides."

"Pretty talk, goth-boy. Pretty talk isn't going to save your life."

His eyes popped open and their deep blue color was almost ebony as they shone intensely. "You already have, my M.J."

She smiled as tears flooded her eyes and her heart lurched in a way she'd only read about in books. "Enough with the romance, goth-boy. Let's see if you feel the same way when I'm not the only one in the world willing to take care of you."

"I should be the one to see to your needs."

"Well, those are words I've never heard before," she muttered.

"Then I shall endeavor to repeat and prove them from now until the end of time."

"Hush you, if you keep up with the sweet words you'll turn my head. Then I won't get to—" M.J. stopped talking when she saw his eyes had closed. Brushing her hand over his forehead she bit back a curse when she realized he was colder. Crap. He might as well be a corpse. "Don't die," her whisper was part plea and part prayer. "Please, please, please. Just don't die."

Which was when things got worse.

His body was suddenly covered with sweat, but not in any normal-I-have-a-really-high-fever kind of way. This was as if his body had turned on a faucet at full blast and nothing could stop it. His clothing quickly became soaked, and still it came. M.J. rushed back to the carts and grabbed two stacks of towels someone had the foresight to supply. She packed them around him, but still the water came. Sitting back on her heels, M.J.'s mouth fell open as she watched the fluid overrun the towels and begin to pool around him. "Pool?" Looking up at the tile walls surrounding them and the open drain she wondered if this was less a case of his friends not caring about his welfare, and more an issue of her not understanding what she'd been kidnapped into.

What in hell had she walked into?

Aquos groaned, and she tried to brush his hair back, but it was like trying to mold water. Her eyes moved over the perfection of his face, absorbing the sculpting of his features and the way they fit together. He was so fine. Like something Michelangelo would create, not a guy who'd go for plain-Jane M.J. Storm.

What a joke.

Coughing harshly, M.J. braced his shoulders against the pool float as best she could. Flinging off the blankets she recognized they were no longer going to help. The water coming out of him was icier than his skin.

He was going to die.

"Listen to me," she yelled to the ceiling, "I need help. I don't want him to die. Help me save him." Leaning her head against his face, she longed to blow the heat from her frame into him. To give him breath. Her lips brushed against his, and he seemed to respond. It was a fleeting gentle brush of their mouths, lighter than the sensation of a butterfly's wings.

But it was enough.

It had to be.

Standing up, she tapped her fingers against her leg. "I'll get help."

Rushing to the door, she peeked out through the opening. Her heart thundered in her chest so hard she covered it with her hand. Panic would not save him. Straightening her back, she repeated the one thing that had guided her through countless bad foster families and too many nightmarish group homes. "I am M.J. Storm and nothing's keeping me down."

The lights in the hall to the left flickered. *Finally.* Some help.

When she made it half way down the corridor, another twinkle in the sconces told her where to go. "Ok, read your mind intercom system, you keep lighting the way, and I'll follow. Just please make sure it's to someone who can save him."

Three more turns and she finally stopped. In front of her was another person, only she seemed to be hiding from something, not running to her to help. M.J. froze as she witnessed a woman who was everything she was not. Dressed in a man's cast off white button down shirt, she wore a dusky rose skirt that went to the floor. Her hair looked the same strawberry color you only see in fairy tale books, face beautiful, delicate and feminine from her head to her toes.

M.J. really wanted to hate her for that alone.

"Hello," she spoke loudly to get the stranger's attention since she was so busy walking on her tiptoes and looking behind her with a guilty expression.

The girl jumped a mile into the air, gave her a startled look. "Hello. Who are you?"

"I'm M.J. sorry to bother you, especially since you seem to be escaping from something or someone ..." M.J. really hoped the monster wasn't coming after the girl since she didn't have time to kill someone while she was busy trying to save Aquos's life. "I really need your help."

"Who brought you here?"

"Tall guy, looks constipated, and a mean left hook."

"One of my boys hit you?" She took a few steps closer and cupped M.J.s face in her hand. "Where? I'm Sally by the way."

"You can see the bruise," she pointed out. "Nice to meet you. Listen, I really don't have time for this, my pain is nothing, I need to ..." Sally seemed to brush something soothing against her face and the pain disappeared. "What'd you do?"

"Healed you, silly. Now, what other help did you need?"

"Aquos," M.J. grabbed Sally's hand and pulled. "You have to help me save him."

 11

Her hand clasped to the girl's, M.J. kept pulling her as she ran back to her patient. "I'm sorry," she told her. "I just ... I don't know what I'm doing, and this illness is beyond anything I've ever seen. When someone gets a fever, they sweat or at least you want them to, but this is just not normal. And he's so cold. No one can live who's that cold. I'd really like him to live."

"It's ok," Sally squeezed her fingers with her free hand. "These guys are never normal. We'll figure it out."

They made it back to the room, and M.J. cursed when she saw Aquos' raft was now floating. Even the open drain wasn't allowing the fluid build-up from pooling to exit. "There's not normal, and then there's that." Her heartbeat thundered in her chest, filling her ears with a whooshing sound. "What the hell am I looking at right now?"

"Oh my. It's transpotheosis, but I never thought to see Aquos do it." Sally took her by the shoulders. Her steady, calming eyes seemed to reach into M.J.'s chest and made her heart calm. "None of that matters, M.J. At its truest heart, what you're looking at is Aquos, a man who needs you."

"Why do you think that matters?"

The beautiful stranger smiled, and M.J. could see something wistful and dreamy fill her eyes. "Because it mattered to me as soon as I met my husband, and I was as shocked as you are right now when it did."

"What do I do?"

"Take a deep breath and go with it," Sally said.

Rushing over to him, M.J. immediately began to shiver as she moved through the water. Her mangled skirt trailed around her, long past any hope of repair. When she reached Aquos' side, she cried out softly as his chilled skin was easy to feel before she even touched him. "Go with it? If I leave him here, he's going to freeze to death. My love life is cold enough as it is, I don't want a guy who's solid ice." M.J. ignored Sally's bark of laughter as she soothed his hair back from his head. She would swear she could see ice crystals in his eye lashes already. "How do I help him?"

Sally took his other side and put her hands on Aquos' chest. She cocked her head to the side, took her hands off him, and shook them. This time she put one hand on his neck and the other on his arm. Again she took them away and shook. "This should work." Back-and-forth she did this, over and over, six times. When whatever she was waiting, or looking for, still didn't happen, she cursed softly. "It always works." Looking at M.J., for the first time her confident expression began to crumble and despair started to peak through. It almost made M.J. feel better, it certainly matched what she was feeling. "Aquos," Sally shook him. "Aquos, wake up."

Nothing.

Just more water pouring out of every inch of his skin. His float was now up to their mid-chests, her legs were numb with cold, her fingers turning blue.

"Aquos," Sally yelled louder.

He just moaned and tossed on his raft.

"You try."

M.J. bit her lip "Aquos?" She jostled him on his pillow, "Aquos, wake up."

His eyes opened. "My-M.J.," he whispered before another round of coughing. "You have a need?"

When he tried to get up, she held him down on the raft, concerned he was going to drown. "Easy does it, goth-boy. Sally needs you."

"Drake's Sally?"

"Just Sally," she corrected him. When he turned to her, she smiled at him and M.J. had to resist the urge to dump him in the water. *Jerk.* "Aquos, how do we help you?"

"Can't. No help. No hope."

"There's always hope," looking at M.J., Sally motioned to Aquos, "you tell him."

"Hope is always a step away," M.J. breathed in her hands to warm them and tried to cup his face. "If we could just get you warm …" She looked around the cavernous chamber and inwardly shrugged. "Is there a hot tub or Jacuzzi in this mansion? Or even better … one outside?"

"Of course," they both answered.

"Let's take him there." When both looked at her like she was crazy, she started to pull him from the raft. He had to help her before she saw progress. "This place isn't warming you up and the cold isn't doing any of us any good. I don't look good in blue, goth-boy. So we might as well try something else."

Sally stepped over to them and fitted her body under his arm. With both of them on either side, they managed to get him out of the pool and headed toward the door. Aquos suddenly stiffened, removed his body from Sally's support. "This is not proper," he announced with surprising formality. "Drake's Sally, you are growing his young. I cannot rely on you to assist me through this bout of illness when we have no way of knowing how it might affect your child. The future prince must be protected."

"Aquos—"

"You're a Queen?" Sally screeched. "I'm so sorry I touched you."

"What's wrong with touching me?"

"Isn't it rude or disrespectful?"

"Don't be ridiculous," Sally waved her hands. "Besides, I touched you first."

"We'd never be able to carry him far anyway," M.J. pointed out. Looking at the carts the robed figures had left, she smiled as a crazy idea hit her. Clearly time with Squirt was rubbing off on her. That sounded as dangerous as it felt. "Maybe if we put him on one of these ... how far is this hot tub?"

"It's right outside the east wing patio doors."

"That come with a map, Magellan?"

Sally laughed, "End of the hall toward the left."

"Think this will work?"

"Definitely."

M.J. was so shocked at her confidence she had to ask, "Why?"

"No other choice," Sally shrugged. "So it has to."

"Super."

"How did you get the elementals to bring so much stuff?" Sally asked.

"I yelled out the request and in came the carts."

"That's weird," Sally said. When M.J. gave her a confused look she hastily explained. "I was told they only respond to certain ... members of the families who live here."

"Not the problem right now, I hope you're stronger than you look."

Sally just gave her a slow, smug smile.

The two of them managed to get the barely conscious man onto the cart. With Sally holding him steady, M.J. positioned herself to push. "You're going to have to navigate." Her first push did little but send her slipping across the floor. "What's he made of ... stone?"

"Water," Sally answered. Pointing to the flood still pouring from him, "See?"

"Great. I'm stuck with a dying goth-boy and a queen who looks like she belongs on the cover of a fashion magazine."

"You think I look like a fashion model?" Sally beamed at her, then scowled. "Aquos is not going to die."

"What makes you say that?"

"Because we won't let him. He's my husband's best friend, Drake would be sad if he died."

Somehow, M.J. knew that to Sally, anything that would upset her husband was forbidden. She couldn't help but wonder just what kind of lightweight man this delicate creature had married.

"Then you'd better push," she suggested to her new friend. When Aquos shuddered through another of those horrible hacking cough attacks, she didn't have to tell the other girl twice. Together, they put everything behind their shove to the cart, which finally began to move. As they traveled over the tile floor, M.J. sent a silent prayer to the heavens to help speed them on their way.

Of course, why she did it confused her, since it had never worked before.

12

By the time they reached the doors, M.J. was so tired she just wanted to lie down in the hallway and take a nap. The problem was they left a trail of water so wide, she'd be soaked in minutes and it would probably give her pneumonia. Looking at Sally, she scowled. Her new friend, however, appeared as fresh and together as she had been when she first saw her. "Aren't you tired? Pushing this cart isn't like taking a walk around a supermarket."

"I have ... unexpected depths."

"What's that mean?"

"My child might be giving me additional reserves."

"How about explaining for the girls in the cheap seats?"

Sally bit her lip as she took a long slow breath in. "Let's just say, I'm not what I look like."

M.J. gestured to the still leaking man on the cart and the river they left behind their wake. "Seems as if no one is here."

"You'd be surprised."

"Not really. My life hasn't exactly been a page out of Norman Rockwell's calendar."

"Preach it, sister."

The two women shared a chuckle as they worked together to push the cart over the bumpy patio tile. When they got to the edge of the hot tub, it was a simple task to spin the cart, so Aquos' feet were hanging into the water. "I'll get the heaters started," Sally offered.

Cupping his face in her hands, M.J. brushed her thumbs over his cheeks.

The water streaming from his pores was still icy and made her skin chill. He opened his eyes and gave her a sad, tired smile. "Hey there, goth-boy. We got you this far, but now I'm going to need you to help me out. Can you move yourself into the hot tub? I was going to just slide you in, but I'm worried you'll hit your head."

"My M.J.," a hacking cough shook him so hard she could feel it under her feet. "I would leap buildings for you, should you ask."

"Big talk again, goth-boy, let's just start with the hot tub."

He moved slowly, as if weights were holding him down, but still managed to slide into the tub as she asked. "I will soon overflow this."

"I know," M.J. gestured to the nearby lawn. "The grass will take care of it."

"The water's going to get hot fast," Sally looked up from the controls. "I put it up as high as it goes."

"Good," M.J. smiled when Aquos looked at her, one eyebrow raised. *Crap. Why was that expression the cutest thing she'd ever seen?* This man was way too dangerous to her. "I think you need heat."

"Heat is all I feel when I gaze at you."

"Like I said ... big talk, goth-boy." M.J. started to pull the towels left on the cart. She rolled them up and placed them in the small shelf surrounding the tub to hopefully create a dam for the water. This activity kept her looking down so no one could see her blush.

"You're about the color of a cooked lobster," Sally whispered in her ear.

"Shut it," she turned to Sally, happy to give Aquos her back. "That's no one's business."

"Well," Sally smiled. "No one just passed out and is about to drown."

"Crap." Whirling around, she dove for the tub. M.J. wrapped her arms around his upper chest and managed to get him turned upright. Half of her was in the tub, but at least his face was no longer a few inches under the water line. "You could help. Aren't you the one with the surprising depths?" she asked Sally.

"Nope. Sorry." Sally was backing away from her. "I think you two are going to be just fine."

M.J. watched in shock as the other woman went skipping back to the house. *Skipping.* She could hunt her down and kill her, if letting Aquos go wouldn't be a guarantee to kill him. "This place is nuts," she shared to her insensate patient. Sighing, she managed to get the rest of her body into the water with him. At least the heat from the hot tub was helping lighten the freeze from his body. Jostling him, she got Aquos' head on her shoulder and tightened her arms around his chest. She'd never been a pillow for a hot guy before ... or even, any guy. It was kind of nice. She wasn't just his pillow; she was more like a chair for him at the moment. He smelled amazing, and the water was getting the dust off quite nicely from her I-just-can't-resist-polishing session on her latest project . Another bonus was they were both more comfortable now. The bench was wide enough for his butt to fit on it as well. Nestling her face against his cheek, she smiled. "This is probably the best date I've ever been on."

"Good," the rumbly purr he gave was something she felt from head to toe. "I wish to be your best everything."

"Rest, goth-boy. I'm not doing a drowned rat impersonation for just anyone."

"If you are unhappy to be here—"

"Aquos," her arms tightened around him to keep him from withdrawing his body from her hold. "I'm fine. I'm glad I'm here so I can help. Your friends are certainly not doing you any good."

He shook his head then rested it against her again. "It is my duty to care for you, not the other way around."

"You'd be the first to have that opinion."

The bitterness in her voice was so thick it gained his attention. When he turned his tired eyes to her, she swallowed back a sob. "M.J. ..."

"Rest, goth-boy. Just rest."

"When I am well, I swear I shall find each of the cretins who put the pain in your eyes and drown them slowly."

"From what I've read, drowning tends only to come slowly."

"I can make it last for centuries."

His growly voice made something deep within her flutter in response. "Big talk again, goth-boy. Close your eyes."

"I shall not always do as you command."

M.J.'s soft laughter was the only response he received but it was enough to send him into slumber with a smile upon his face.

13

Sally piled the pickles on the slices of raw meat, slapped some cheese on top, rolled it together and started to chew. *This baby was going to kill her.* She'd never wanted to eat meat in her entire life, and now she couldn't seem to get enough of it. Not to mention the pickles, little bombs of pure delicious salty goodness. As the flavors combined, bursting on her tongue, she moaned with joy. The baby seemed to do the same, settling for the first time in hours as he recognized she was finally giving him what it needed. Screw needed. This prince knew how to demand.

Even though he was still in her womb.

"I warned you that your disgust of flesh would eventually be overruled by the life growing within you."

She scowled as she continued to make more of the roll-ups, ignoring the male standing behind her, clearly passing judgment. "Tamar."

"My liege …"

"Go home."

"I fear I cannot."

"Why is that?"

"You have experienced your first kanji. Your dragon is quickening, my Queen. It is my sworn duty to be by your side until the King is hatched."

Grimacing, Sally tried to push away the disgust she felt every time the dragons used the word *hatched.* It just felt so wrong. Somehow she was supposed to give birth to an egg, as if that wouldn't give her alien-like nightmares every day for the rest of her life … but she was expected to pop out an egg, and then give it to Drake to watch for a whole year until the baby within was ready to break the shell and be officially born. *On one hand … no midnight feedings. But on the other hand … no midnight feedings.* She felt both blessed and cheated at the same exact time. Turning, she realized that not only was Tamar intruding on her private just-let-me-eat-in-peace moment, but he'd brought a friend. "Hello Hunter. Tamar, you seem to be slacking. Why is Hunter here and not guarding the portal?"

"Others have been given this task."

"So why are you here?" She tried to push away her desire to throw the food in her hands at the intruders. If she did, she wouldn't be able to eat it, and right now, she really wanted her child to stop kicking her inner organs. Women should be warned, when they hit puberty, what motherhood was really like. No girl would ever fall in love again, or at least not have sex. *This baby had better be freaking adorable.* She was eating actual meat, raw meat at that. Taking a big bite, she gestured to the two men. "Speak up. Your Queen demands it."

"I find it humorous that you call yourself Queen only when you wish us to do something that is against our law."

"There's a law that the two of you have to bug me?" Hunter flinched as if she'd struck him. She let out a sigh and held up her hands. *Rudeness was not royal.* Or at least it wasn't in her book. "Forgive me." Sally took a large bite of the meat, and patted her stomach. "A hungry baby makes a hangry Queen."

"Hangry?"

"Hungry and angry. It's an Earth thing."

The two men nodded as if they understood what she was saying, even though their eyes clearly reflected confusion. "Why are you here, Tamar? You never leave the limbo lands lightly, and you wouldn't pull Hunter off the portal unless something was seriously wrong. So please explain this to me."

"My Queen, your dragon is quickening. The future King grows stronger."

Sally pushed away the impulse to censure him for forgetting her command that he stop calling her Queen. It was like he was trying to remind her, and irritating as hell. Technically, she'd started it this time. But seriously, in all those princess dreams she'd had as a child, she'd never imagined it would be such a headache in reality. "I know my dragon and the prince are quickening, Tamar. I can feel it."

"I must be in attendance to assist you at all times. It is my blood oath to our King and our people."

"And Hunter?"

"He is still the best choice to be your mate."

"Please. Not this again. You officiated my wedding to Drake."

"I did. But this does not change the fact that Hunter is the one who was destined to be your—"

A roar echoed through the halls of Sanctuary and reached the kitchen where they stood. It seemed a living thing, as if a mighty bird trapped indoors, bouncing against the walls and windows in eternal torment. "Super." Sally took another huge bite as she rubbed her free hand on her stomach. "Drake's up."

It took a few more minutes for her husband to find them. Sally continued to eat as her eyes were pinned to the two males standing before her. Tamar, with his black and silver hair and piercing obsidian eyes, and Hunter, with his tousled blond hair and sage-green eyes; neither of them realizing just how vicious Drake could be when pushed. Their bodies were straight off a classic romance book cover; she suspected they were also sharp as tacks and even passionate. In a strange detached manner, she could even imagine they were great in bed. But nothing, and no one, could ever hold a candle to her husband, Drake.

Her enraged gorgeous husband, who was standing in the doorway. "Food?"

"That plus Aquos' and his new friend, M.J., needed some help."

"My Queen," Hunter gave her what should have been a devastatingly charming smile, but really only made her roll her eyes. "Allow me to stay and serve you. I am determined to prove myself."

She sighed. *Seriously? She was growing a human, well, a new life at least; she didn't need this drama.* "Hunter, cut it out. You're a friend, no more. I've no interest in a second husband, this one is more than enough. Tamar, if you make waves in my home, I'll have Aquos drown you. Drake, stop thinking of all the ways you can kill these two. We don't make messes for the elementals to clean inside the house."

"I can kill them outside."

"There are other things happening outside, and we should probably do something about them."

"How, Sally-mine, shall we resolve your advisor's issue?"

"Yes, Tamar. How should we resolve your problem with my husband?"

"I vote I pull out their entrails and tie them into bows for you."

Sally was going to take another bite, but at Drake's graphic suggestion she tossed the meat to the side. "Gross." Without a word, Drake went and got her the large bowl of blueberries the elementals had taken to keeping in the refrigerator just for her. For whatever reason, they were the only thing that calmed her stomach in these moments. He handed it to her and she shoved a handful in her mouth. "See?" Her full mouth was easily cleared with a swallow. Sally took the time to consume three more handsful before continuing. "Drake is the perfect husband for me, Tamar. He has my heart. Please stop putting me into the position where I have to worry about him having you killed as gruesomely as he can imagine. Am I being clear?"

"Yes, my Queen."

"And Hunter?"

"How may I serve you, my Queen?"

"Put the flirty smiles away. They're pissing me off."

"By your command."

Sally sighed. "And if you guys have another science fiction television marathon without me, I'm gonna hand Drake the weapons to speed his severing all of your limbs. Am I being perfectly clear?"

"I wouldn't need weapons," Drake snorted.

"Yes, honey. I know you've got the biggest one in the room."

"Biggest what?"

"Nothing," all three responded to Hunter's inquiry at once.

"Tamar, find Hunter a room in our tower--"

"Main part of the house," Drake interrupted.

Right. Because her dragon couldn't stand the thought of other dragons being around his dragon. But dragons loved the air so being up in the tower would be more polite. *Eh. Screw it*. She may be queen, but right now she was playing the pregnancy card. Poor Drake. After all that time of being on the outs with his clan ... he was stuck with a million of these annoyances a day. To think there had been a time Drake had believed he was the last dragon left alive.

"In the morning, you two should go home."

"We cannot, my Queen."

Drake's eyes were piercing as they examined both men's faces. "Why is that?"

"My apologies if you are unaware of our traditions, consort." Tamar spoke stiffly, his face shuttering.

"No one taught me."

Sally sighed. *Those two were going to be no help*. She turned to Hunter, hoping one male member of the species would have a lick of sense. "Hunter, why do you guys need to stay here?"

"While you grow our King, my Queen, it is tradition that there be an honor guard in constant attendance. Leaving would upset the kachi required for your dragonswan. Balance must be maintained."

"Ok, kachi?"

"Their presence keeps your dragon self in stasis. It prevents the transpotheosis from happening so the child within can grow in safety."

Sally stepped over to Drake and shut her eyes when his arms instantly closed around her. She felt the tension ease that had gripped her since Tamar and Hunter had entered. It was always the way with her and Drake. Whatever felt broken, or less than without him, was lightened with just the touch of his hands. *Tamar was right. Bastard usually was*. Her dragon had come more regularly and started to fight her for control. Sex with Drake helped, but if the others had heard of the struggle, she understood that even that might not be enough soon. She didn't want to be afraid, but some truths were hard to escape. The world of dragons was sensual, powerful, and unfortunately, quite deadly. It was impossible not to have it get to her.

"You will be fine, Sally-mine."

"I always am, with you."

"We will find our own accommodations," Tamar announced.

"Not too close to our lair."

"Very well."

"I'm sure the elementals will help," Sally said.

"Our appreciation," they chorused as they left.

"Drake?"

He brushed his lips across her forehead. Then the tip of her nose, and finally her mouth. Her toes curled in her slippers, her hands tightened into fists into the back of his shirt. When he broke away from her, both of their breaths were harsh panting gasps. "We'll be fine, Sally. I swear it. And our child shall be brought into a world of love and acceptance."

"Right. What world is that exactly?"

"The one we make ourselves, whether it is inside these walls or without."

"Right," she shook her body to try and cast off some of the sensual fugue Drake was an expert at building around her, just by breathing. "Speaking of without, we should probably talk about Aquos."

"What about him? The fact that he's sick again or his ongoing crush on you?"

"His girlfriend."

When his eyebrow rose and his mouth fell open, Sally laughed loudly. Drake was frozen, just staring at her, his mind clearly blown. It was perfect. One man competing to be her husband, when she was already married, didn't faze him. Another dragon trying to take control of their child didn't stun her mate. But his best friend finally getting his own girl could leave him gobsmacked.

For all the chaos this place seemed to run on, there was one thing you could always count on here.

Things were never boring in Sanctuary.

14

Aquos felt good. It had been so long since he'd felt good he wasn't even sure what it was at first. He was floating, the water a sensual embrace for his entire body. His temperature was normal. He even felt warm. There was no pain, no problem breathing, no crippling cramps hitting his arms and legs.

He actually felt good.

The hot tub was smaller than what he usually preferred during one of the attacks. He didn't remember choosing it, now he wondered what had taken him so long. The twenty-person tub had been a joke from the Speed Clan, after a particular bad betting period during the turn of the century. He should thank them. Stretching out his limbs, he turned his senses to the water embracing him.

Looking up, he could identify his favorite constellation, Orion. It was close to one he'd been raised to scope while wandering through the oceans as a child in Omega. He called to the energy in the water and had it move through him to fill all those empty spaces he'd been burdened with for so long. Then he felt it. Something new. An element he'd never detected before, binding to the cells deep within him, bringing a calm to the magic that allowed him to be who he was for the first time in his adult years. It was simply and utterly glorious. Rising from the water, he planned on yelling to his brothers to tell of his good fortune.

As he raised his upper body from the fluid, he saw a woman. Floating in the tub beside him, her long burgundy colored hair undulating with the movement of the liquid, looking like someone had spilled a glass of fine wine.

M.J. *Why was she swimming?* Aquos turned her over, not understanding what he was seeing. *Why she was so still?* Her lips were edged in blue, a gray cast to the coffee color of her skin. He shook her a little, hoping he'd get some movement in response. Hear her call him, "Goth-boy," with that teasing tone. He called to the energy in her body trying to understand what was afflicting his woman. The water. It was swimming through her lungs, her stomach, her throat even.

It took little more than a thought to demand the fluid leave her body. He tried to make her as close to Sally as he could remember, from the one time he had tried to help heal Drake's mate after she'd been poisoned. Sally had water in her, but not clogging up certain organs. Aquos called to it, drying what was left as best as he knew how. Then he sent a small jolt to M. J.'s heart so it would beat as Sally's did. M.J. was in his arms when she took her first free breath. He nestled his face in her neck, enjoying the way the air felt against his cheek as her chest rose and fell. Her smell was spice and chocolate, turning his body into molten need. The warmth of the hot tub began to soak into her as well, turning her blue skin to the normal coffee that was so fetching with her hair and snapping eyes.

She came back to him.

"Ah ... quos." His name rolled from her lips as a sigh, and it turned his body rock hard before the second syllable cleared her lips.

"Just breathe, my love."

"Aquos, kiss me." She moved over his body, her knees on either side of his legs, her hands sliding over his pecs, around his neck to spear into his hair and still his head. "Kiss me, my Aquos."

Pushing away the concern at her sudden change, and his surge of good fortune, Aquos stopped fighting her. No one had ever called him stupid; he was not about to start proving otherwise. Their lips came together like a sudden summer storm, strong, skirting the line almost to violence. Tongues dueling, her taste was sweet innocence with a trace of seduction. His arms pulled her closer to his body and he groaned into her mouth when he felt her breasts push into his chest. She was still in control, her hips undulating against his straining rock hard erection. Her fingers buried in his hair as she turned his head the direction she wanted.

It was the hottest thing that ever happened to him in his extremely long, lonely life.

One of her hands stayed speared in his hair, keeping his face angled so she could kiss him more deeply. The other began desperately to fumble with his pants, and he was happy to rip them open for her. His hands returned to her hip and back, only there to steady her. She was in control, and he liked it that way. His entire body was throbbing in time to the pulsing need of his erection, but he just wanted to see where she was going to take this. Aquos was happy for the ride … though he hoped he was about to provide her with one of her own.

When she began to undulate against him, he tore his mouth away from her so he could groan. She pulled the collar of his shirt to the side and nipped the small patch of skin. Aquos cupped her core feeling her heat through the water and clothing, M.J. threw her head back. "Yes. More."

His fingers worked her clit through the fabric guarding her. She shook her head. "Skin-to-skin."

Shrugging, *since what man would refuse such a request*, Aquos ripped her panties in two. "My-M.J. are you sure about this?"

"Never more sure." M.J. seemed lost in her own fog of sensual need. He was so unused to women of this time, choosing rarely to leavie the compound, and only interacting with the humans on their Halloween. He'd never known a female would be this bold, this clear on what she wanted and when she expected it. Even Mach and Turbo had neglected to tell him that women could be … this … incredibly … sexy.

He loved it.

Again she moved, rising from the water by leveraging her hands against his shoulders. Her folds brushed over his straining dick and his groan was loud enough to wake the scouts in the forest surrounding the house. She was hotter and wetter than the tub surrounding them. When she got the tip lodged in her channel and began to circle her hips, he felt as if he had let her take the lead for long enough. Aquos was determined to prove her wisdom in picking him. His strength had returned, and this woman was about to experience the benefit of a Water Clan's power.

His left arm banded around her hips, as he speared his fingers into her hair so he could give her that slight bite of pain. With a call to the water, he steadied her body and pulled her down until he was seated to the hilt. He heated her from the inside out, the fluid within her body answering his call. The hands she had tangled in his hair began to tug, trying to force him into moving, quickening the pace he meticulously set. Again, he wondered what sane man would ever refuse a woman who wanted him so much she demanded immediate release.

His hands around her tightened. Her body didn't know how to achieve the angles it needed or what pace to get the release she was demanding. It was easy enough for him to provide. As he moved her up and down his shaft with his arm around her hips, his other hand steadied itself on her front, keeping her pressure on the precious bundle of nerves so key to a woman's fulfillment. She wanted to get off fast; he planned on being there with her each step of the way. When his control broke, it didn't just crack, it shattered into a million pieces. His body was now responding to its own list of demands. The faster she moved up and down, the harder he pushed against her clit. He managed to capture her lips and took her desperate breathy gasps into his mouth and deep in his soul, right where they belonged.

When he came, he felt as if his entire being shot out from him into the heart of this fiery woman in his arms. Her release was just as overwhelming. Her scream pierced the night sky, bringing a smile to his lips. It was her choice to bend her head and take his lips. Their tongues dueling, breaths combining, her taste imprinting itself into the deepest recesses of his being.

As the tremors shaking her to her core slowly subsided, M.J. just melted into him. Her head nestled in the crook of his neck, her arms loosely draped over his back. He regretted that in the haste and force of their need, he hadn't taken the time he wanted to savor her. He hadn't even touched her breasts. That was a regret he would not allow to stand for long. Brushing a kiss against her cheek, he slowly pulled her from his body to cradle her against his chest. "You, my M.J., are truly a perfection I did not know possible in this world." He couldn't stop pressing his lips to her face. Her forehead. Her cheek. The tip of her nose. Her long hair made candy red ribbons in the water around them. At first that was where he thought all the color had come from, but then he realized she was bleeding.

Fuck. What had he just done?

His concern was mirrored when M.J.'s head snapped up and she looked at him with wide, tear-filled eyes. She whispered, "What did I do?" before she choked off a sob of horror.

 15

"I just want to check on them."

"Sally-mine, no one here expects you to heal us all of the time. Your first priority must be our young. Even the great Ser Tamar agrees with this pronouncement. Aquos would be the last of our group—"

"You mean family," she corrected him.

Drake pulled his wife into his arms so he could kiss her. It wasn't until after she was in a dazed panting fog that he released her. "Family. Aquos would be the last of our family to ever ask you to exhaust yourself over concern for him. Now … should we not return to our chamber and you to bed?"

"I am not tired."

He kept his tongue still when his first instinct was to argue her point. He'd read the human book on pregnancy several times, and he knew that women needed rest. He was positive that the twenty minutes at a time that Sally managed to sneak out of their bed was detrimental to her health. Tamar agreed with Sally's need to grow their child here, rather than in the dragon limbo lands, and he thoroughly sided with him on the necessity of her staying in bed. Unfortunately, getting Sally to agree was decidedly more difficult. She seemed to feel that males telling her how to grow young was rude. "If you have no desire to sleep, there are other ways I could keep you entertained."

"That's what left me with swollen ankles and a constant desire to eat pickles with peanut butter and raw meat."

"Shall I fetch it for you?" Getting his woman food sounded much better than watching her track Aquos.

"No, Drake. Right now we're checking on Aquos who is ill and M.J. who's terrified."

"How would you know she's terrified?"

"I saw her face. Her bruised face. Wait … where's Turbo?"

"Why do you need to see Turbo?" He scowled. Sally's comfort at spending time with his brothers was both gratifying and disturbing to his peace of mind. Dragonswans don't spend time with males when breeding, a fact his woman seemed determined to ignore. Of course, his woman was also the dragon queen, so he couldn't really make her do anything, though he enjoyed trying to convince her with every tool in his sensual arsenal … speaking of which … "Why don't we go back to our room?"

"Turbo, Drake. Where is Turbo?"

"I have no idea, Sally-mine. I am hardly his keeper."

"He hit her, Drake."

"Why do you care so much about this female?"

"She's a woman, Drake. Women should always try to help each other. This is important to me."

"Then it's important to me," he hugged her close to his body, sending the command to his form to not respond to her softness. "I will address Turbo and his treatment of females in the morning, my heart. Please trust me."

"I do."

"Can we please go back to bed?"

"Of course not," she slipped out of his hold and pranced down the hall. "There's still Aquos to deal with."

He sighed. *Seriously?* He had never dared to dream he would find a woman of such inner and outer beauty, but if he had, he was sure he would never have thought she would be so hard to control. The dragon cave in the limbo lands was sounding more and more attractive. At least there he could demand the males of their species keep their distance. Looking up through the plate glass windows, his eyebrows rose in shock. "Somehow, my heart, I do not feel Aquos would appreciate us intruding."

"Why not?"

"Look."

Her gasp did not herald their return to their chamber. Instead, she ran outside.

16

Aquos was stunned when M.J. jumped out of the hot tub and ran from the patio. He didn't know what just happened. He'd just had the best sex of his life and the creature who had almost blown his mind with pleasure was running away from him with tears in her eyes. This wasn't something the Speed cousins warned him about. He didn't know if he should go after her, beat the crap out of himself ... or possibly both. Drake and Sally passed M.J. as she fled.

"I'll go check on her."

"Thank you," Aquos called after Sally as she rushed after M.J.

"Anything you would care to discuss?"

He rose from the water and stretched. Aquos couldn't believe how much better he felt. He could feel the energy pulsing through his cells, every inch of his skin responding to the magic suddenly surging in him. If sex in the water could give him this much of a surge of health, he was going to start to jack—

"Buddy?"

His eyes snapped to Drake's face and he chuckled. "Is this what it was like when you first met Sally?"

Drake smiled and tossed a towel at him. "You mean, did I feel like I was drunk on ambrosia as much as I felt beaten to within an inch of my lives?"

"Pretty much."

"Sums it up nicely."

"Good to know." Aquos tossed the towel to the side and instead used his powers to dispel the water from his hair and skin. His powers. He hadn't had such access to his abilities since he was a child. Stretching his fingers, he flicked his wrist and heard a crack of thunder before the lightning lit the yard. Power. He'd actually forgotten what it felt like. *What else could he do?*

"Buddy?"

This time when he met Drake's smile, he chuckled. "Sorry. I don't know what just happened."

"Smells like you guys had sex."

"Yeah. Never tell her you can do that."

"Why?"

"No offense, dragon, but I'm pretty sure humans have issues with those type of senses."

"So Sally tells me."

"You didn't believe her?"

"I always believe my woman. Understanding her rarely occurs, but I'm usually just so grateful she lets me near her, I'll do whatever she says."

Aquos waved his hand again, instantly clearing the patio of the standing water. The return of his powers was seriously coming in handy. "Sounds like a good plan. Any clue on why she ran from here crying? We just had the most amazing sex of my life and she's crying. I don't understand, Drake. Is it a human thing?"

"Sally cries, but not usually after sex."

"Great. You're no help."

The return of his wife made the dragon turn around and immediately wrap his arms around her. This is what Aquos had wanted since the first time he'd seen Sally. The bond between husband and wife was as tangible in the room as the furniture and floor. Whenever they were near each other, they were touching or watching their spouse. He realized that Drake was responding to Sally's proximity as much as to her upset. It had to be bad news. The sight of Drake's hands cupping Sally's rounded stomach where their child was growing sent a bolt of pure longing through him so intense it almost sent him to his knees.

"What ails you, Sally-mine?"

"She wouldn't talk to me."

"I'll make her," Drake turned to pursue M.J., but Sally grabbed his arm to keep him close. "I won't make her?"

"No, honey. It doesn't work that way."

Aquos watched the two of them argue with a smile. "Can you guess why she's crying?"

"I'm sorry, Aquos. What happened before we came out?"

Drake started to laugh and Aquos reconsidered his need for a best friend. Tamar would never allow Sally to stay unmarried for long, so at least that wouldn't be a problem. She'd get over the loss eventually.

"Nothing."

Sally didn't seem to appreciate or believe his stiff answer so she turned to her hyena of a husband. "They were intimate," he managed to choke out.

"Oh. Well," a slight pink filled her cheeks. "Maybe she didn't like it?"

"She did." Aquos scowled now considering a desire to murder both of them.

"Are you sure?" Drake tilted his head to the side. "These human females can sometimes act like—"

Sally elbowed her husband as Aquos interrupted his reply.

"I said," Aquos scowled. "She liked it. I was paying attention, you two. And she was the one who initiated the entire encounter."

"So it was all her doing?"

Aquos shared a smug smile with Drake. "I did help things along."

"Maybe she regretted it?"

He closed his eyes and tried to remember all of the reasons he liked these two people, even loved them. Killing them was not going to feel good in the long run. Suddenly he felt a ripping within his heart, and he looked up in surprise. M.J. Something was wrong. She was no longer safe inside sanctuary and he could feel her terror. Without saying a word to his former friends, Aquos went running as fast as he could toward the waves of panic M.J. emitted.

He might not be killing his friends today, but whoever was scaring his woman, he would happily tear to bits.

17

M.J. ran straight into the arms of the monster. Typical. She must have been born with a danger magnet, not to mention the loser one. The monster was covered with dirt and scratches, there were even some leaves in his hair. When he looked at her he actually growled. Not the sexy growl a girl dreams a guy gives because he wants her so much. This was one of those frightening, soul-curdling sounds that is meant to warn the species that death was imminent.

Holding her hands up, she backed up slowly, "Sorry, buddy. Just passing through here, I mean no harm."

The monster's eyes flashed a yellow green color that definitely screamed you are not in Kansas anymore, Dorothy. M.J. tried to take slow shallow breaths to hide her fear. "We've already tussled. I'm just looking to go home."

"No." The monster's lip curled with distaste. "You stay."

"I've got to go." M.J. was really glad the monster didn't know she'd just raped his friend. "I've really got to go. There's someone at home waiting for me, and I have a ton of work to do. You can't just keep me here."

"You have no permission," the monster folded his arms over his chest. "You stay. I no repeat."

Seriously? Cave man, much? "Buddy, listen, let's just pretend you didn't see me and no talk of kidnapping has to come up." M.J. started to walk past him, but the monster shot his arm out to make her stop. She turned on him. "I have to go home, okay? Now just leave me alone and let me go." M.J. started to inch her way around him, praying he wouldn't stop her.

"You belong here," the Monster went to throw his hands out to gesture to the grounds.

Instead, his fist clipped M.J. in the jaw, sending her body flying.

Looking up at him, she was amazed to watch his expression grow darker.

Which was when Aquos arrived.

Somebody, please kill me.

18

"Wise one," Luke bowed when he felt Gabrielle enter the library. Angels. Who knew they had such a thing for old books?

"Son of Light you have no reason to show obeisance to me. I come as a friend." Her entrance made the light softer, filled the chamber with the scent of flowers, and eased the tightening stress of the last day's events, in spite of the pain he felt. Gabrielle smiled at him, "Now, what is it that ails you this night?"

"I fear we have once more broken the compact."

"Broken? Or bent? You Omega Clan Lords are hard to control ... or keep penned in, for that matter."

"The final judgment is yours to make, of course," Luke stated. He watched as the only female archangel swept into the room. Usually she was dressed in simple designer clothes, but this time she wore a long flowing white gown. It was positively traditional for her. When Gabrielle gave him an arch look, he felt sheepish. "Apologies for staring. This is not your usual attire."

"I was called in for censure."

"What'd you do?"

"At Christmas, I chose to interfere with some events. My peers were not pleased at my actions."

He gave her a smile. "Hard to imagine archangels have a peer review board."

"You would be shocked to learn just how many reviews we receive."

"Really?"

"Humans adore calling out to us during periods of trouble or hardship, and of course condemning us for our inattention at all other times. Each curse creates its own set of paperwork and burdens."

"Sorry to hear it."

"There is perfection in the system ... but occasionally perfection is difficult to live with."

"I understand." Luke grimaced as he remembered his mother and the burdens of being her son.

"Now, what is this compact bending your Clan Lords have done?"

Luke sighed. *Right.* This was a business meeting. Not his favorite kind. When they had arrived on Earth through the portal, the archangels had convened and offered them a set of rules to live by, while they were in this dimension. The largest of the commands had been they never interfere with the course of a human's life. As a rule, they managed to obey. Until Sally. Come to think of it, Sally being brought to Drake had been Turbo's doing as well. He wasn't the type of leader to throw his men into the line of fire, but if push comes to shove he would happily offer up the Speed Clan to the wrath of the heavenly host. "It seems there's a woman ..."

"You took another one?"

"Turbo swears her smell made her a possible mate."

"Which is no reason for him to snatch another of our charges."

"I know, and I assure you we will put the girl back as soon as possible."

Gabrielle reached out and ran her hand over his arm. He believed he could hear the sound of a bubbling brook and smell flowers. "Fret not, Son of Light. Let me speak to the girl first. Then we shall see who needs to be sent where."

"I'll take you to her." Luke gestured for the archangel to follow. He hoped that should Turbo have to take punishment for his own actions, the rest of the Speed Clan would not destroy the compact. Turbo and Mach had been inseparable once. They'd been fighting a great deal lately, but the cousins were closer than anyone he knew. He'd struggled for two thousand years to keep the Clan Lords together.

He would hate to see them destroyed by one man's actions.

19

"Aquos, I'm fine."

He growled at her. She had such a different reaction to his growl over the monster's. M.J.'s eyes widened as her body responded to the aggression and possessiveness shining in his eyes, as if someone just turned her inner thermometer from normal to nuclear. *Shit. That gave new meaning to the word hawt.* "Fine is the one thing you are not," he snarled.

Yes, snarled.

Her toes clenched in the dirt. Right. Where the hell were Squirt's Mom's ugly-assed,super-uncomfortable, shoes? "Your face is bruised from someone's fist. This is the second time I have witnessed such a travesty this night. Your eyes are wide and shiny with tears. Your heart is beating so fast, I fear you'll collapse from a cardiac event. You humans are decidedly fragile." He stomped his way over to her, elbowing the monster away from her side. Aquos covered her galloping heart with his hand and stared deeply into her eyes. "Be calm, my M.J., I am concerned for you."

"My heart isn't beating like that because of the monster." She managed to swallow back her wistful sigh at his smile from this news.

The monster scowled at her over Aquos' shoulder. "Monster? My name's Turbo."

"Monster suits you better," M.J. muttered.

"Dead would also work."

Her mouth dropped open when Aquos turned, positioned himself in front of her, and put his hands on his hips as he stared at his friend. "You physically harmed someone on the grounds of Sanctuary. You physically harmed a female, something we've been trained since birth never to do. And worst of all … you messed with someone I … like!"

The last was delivered with a fast right hook to the jaw that sent Turbo flying into a tree, cartoon-style.

M.J. tried to keep herself from reading anything into Aquos' swallowing awkwardly before he said like. He wasn't swallowing back a more important word. *That would be nuts, right?* They'd just met.

And then there was the small matter of her having taken advantage of him.

She was surprised he even managed to say like without vomiting.

"If you dare to touch her, go near her, or even say her name I will rip you into pieces. Am I being clear here, T? Because I no longer care if I shatter the compact, I only care about her."

M.J. watched as the monster, well, Turbo, dragged himself up from the ground, shook himself off, faced her and Aquos and folded his arms over his chest. Aquos took a step toward the other man, and then growled. Once again, her body quivered in response so hard she had to lock her muscles to keep from stepping closer to him. Again, hawt. "Well?"

"I don't even know her name."

Aquos went to launch himself at the monster. A flash of light went off, and angel-boy jumped to keep the two men from clashing. M.J. had to give the guy credit. Those were some serious Jackie Chan-type moves. Then she saw the woman with him and she had to revise her rising opinion of the guy since he was hanging out with a chick that would make most cover-models cry. In the past, other guys who did the same weren't what she'd call a hero. More like an anti-hero.

"Hold," Luke bellowed. "You both know better."

"I have the right," Aquos said. "He physically harmed a woman. My woman."

M.J. looked down at her feet as a bolt of pain pierced her heart. She shouldn't let him call her that. She was going to have to explain to him that she'd basically raped him. It's not like a man so physically ill could have given consent. Even if it had been her first ever experience. Still, she couldn't resist the pure pleasure of the idea that a man, beautiful on the inside and out, would wish to claim her.

Wait, she's a twenty-first century woman. She doesn't want to be claimed.

Fuck you Susan B. Anthony, she totally wants to be claimed. Or at least she does by this guy. Mrs. Goth-boy has a pleasing ring to it.

This was when she realized that the three men and one drop-dead gorgeous woman were all staring at her. *Shit.* Was she saying any of that out loud? The other woman gave a quick shake of the head and she instantly felt better. "What?"

"Luke asked you if you were well." Aquos stepped closer to her, wrapped his arms around her and ran his hands through her hair. Feeling each inch of her scalp, sending tingles down her spine. "Did you hit your head when Turbo struck you? We should call Raphael; she may need to be healed. Gabrielle can you do anything? Perhaps propel his attendance faster?"

"I'm fine." She pushed Aquos' hands off her head and stepped away from his side.

Which compelled him to pull her back into his body.

The woman, Gabrielle, stepped closer to her, with a strange look on her face.

"Gabrielle, will you please call Raphael?"

"I fear, Son of Light, this is one thing I cannot do."

"Why not?"

It pleased M.J. that this caused Luke, Aquos and even the monster to turn to the woman in surprise. She wasn't good with the full-strength attention thing.

"This creature is not our kind."

"Gabrielle, I beg your pardon, but she's a human."

Huh. Who knew the monster could be polite?

"This creature is Omega, gentlemen. I do not understand of what clan she hails or why she's been living with my charges, but she is most definitely not human. This is not a mistake I can risk."

"What?" Finally. Between the shot to the jaw, exhaustion from having been up for twenty-four hours, horror at perpetrating her first sexual assault—not to mention having sex for the first time, period, or the shock of someone saying that she wasn't human, with a completely serious tone, it was too much for M.J.'s brain. Even as her knees folded, and the peacefulness of the dark greeting her beckoned, she knew Aquos would catch her and keep her safe.

She just wished she'd done the same for him.

 20

Aquos set the still-unconscious M.J. on the couch in the great room. He covered her with a throw, concerned she might be cold after running barefoot through the woods. There was so much he didn't understand. First being, what had made her cry after they had sex? Why had she run away? Why did Gabrielle think she was Omega? How could she be Omega? The women at home had all but died out. Their mothers had been the last ones who'd survived, and none of them had lived through the births of their children, except for Luke's, who'd withdrawn from the world when she'd realized the blight was destroying everything.

It didn't explain M.J. though. How could this one woman be lost and found on this far away rock so many years later?

He brushed a lock of her shiny straight hair from her lips, imagining what her life would have been like if she'd been born on their world. She would have been seen as a treasure to an entire planet of men. Warriors from all corners of the globe would have battled to spend a few moments in her presence. Locks of her hair alone would sell for a king's ransom in the precious market. She would have surpassed the titles of queen and empress.

She would have been everything.

It pained him, but his imagination reminded him of the harshest truth. He would not have been worthy of two minutes of this woman's time in their world.

The water clan was never seen as warriors. Or even … noble.

"What the hell is that?"

Aquos's head snapped up at Turbo's derision. "Mine. This is all you need know."

Drake entered with Sally on his arm. When she saw her friend unconscious on the couch she immediately rushed over. "Is she sick?" Without breaking his stride, Drake punched Turbo hard enough to send him crashing into the wall as he moved to go to stand next to Aquos.

"I know not," Aquos admitted.

"What the hell was that for?" Turbo's roar made Drake just fold his arms over his chest and harrumph.

"Sally-mine wished her new friend avenged."

"Thank you," Aquos said. "But I already handled it."

"I thought we were against fighting," Turbo tested his jaw.

"You break the rules, why shouldn't we?" Luke said.

"Tell me what is amiss?"

Everyone ignored Drake's demand as Sally checked on M.J. "I think she just fainted."

Aquos let out his held breath as the relief surged within him. "Good."

"I repeat ... what the hell is that?" Turbo pointed at M.J.

"Mine. Need we go through this again?"

Turbo shook off Aquos' answer. "How can Gabrielle think she's an Omega? Whose clan does she belong to? Who claims her?"

"I do," They ignored Aquos' two-word declaration.

Luke ran his hand through his hair as he scowled at M.J. as well. "I fear the only one who can tell us is the girl."

"So wake the bitch up."

Aquos didn't give a warning or speak. He launched himself at Turbo, determined to put his fist through the Speed Clan eldest's skull. Turbo met him eagerly. Just when they were about to connect, Luke used his entire body as a battering ram to send Turbo backwards, as Drake caught Aquos around the waist and held him from connecting. "Aquos! What's gotten into you?" his friend asked.

Luke was not as calm. "One move, either of you, make one move, and I'll banish you both. Am I clear?" Aquos struggled to reach Turbo, determined to wipe the smug expression off his face. "Aquos," Luke yelled. "If you're banished, M.J. will be here alone. Is that what you want?"

This stilled him. Drake released Aquos slowly, as if he wasn't sure whether it was a trick. It wasn't. The idea of M.J. without his protection in this place caused him physical pain. According to their most ancient histories, this is how things started to fall apart for the clans. They left their women in unsafe situations. They didn't safeguard the future, in the delusional belief it could take care of itself. They rejoiced in war and conquest, never considering culture. This world with its art and music took his breath away. There was so much beauty here, and he saw it all in this girl.

"I will cry peace," Aquos said. "If Turbo will quit the presence of this woman. She's committed no wrong. He, on the other hand, has been physically abusive twice. He will not have a third opportunity."

"He's right," Luke stated. Drake and Sally both nodded in agreement. "Turbo, leave."

"What if I don't want to?"

Luke shrugged, and with a wave of his hand, Turbo disappeared. *Okay then.* When the Light Clan started showing off their powers you knew shit just got real. Mach came in and froze at the scene before him. "Who are we killing?"

"Turbo might have just died."

"Shit. What the fuck did he do now?" he asked Drake.

"Pissed off Luke."

Mach looked at Luke with a combination of respect and fear. "That's possible?"

"Try it," Luke snapped. Then he sighed, and ran his hand through his hair. At this point, it was starting to look like the Son of Light was electrocuted. "Go check on your cursed cousin, Mach. He should be downstairs in the isolation cell."

"Good place for him," Drake said.

Mach turned to go, for once not feeling the compulsion to make a snarky comment. Luke sighed again, "Mach." The youngest of their group froze, but didn't turn around. "If his attitude isn't better, leave him in there. I don't know what his damage is, but I won't have it jeopardizing the compact ... any more than he already has."

"Understood."

They all watched Mach leave. Aquos almost wished he could go with him. He'd spent thousands of years playing the peacemaker to the Clan Lords. But this was one time he understood his only place was protecting the woman snoring softly on the couch next to him. He tucked the blanket tighter around her shoulders and took the chance to run the back of his hand over the curve of her cheek. She was one perfectly made beauty.

Which was when she swatted at his touch and crinkled her nose.

"Back to the original dilemma. What do we do with the girl?"

"She's a woman," Sally reminded them.

All three men rolled their eyes. This was Sally's new thing. First it was getting them to know the elementals by name rather than by function. Now it was the difference between girls and women.

"My apologies," Luke said. "What do we do with the woman?"

"I want her."

Now all the men stared at Sally.

"Uhm, Sally-mine, I don't really want you to have another mate. Even if she is a female."

"Drake," her cheeks flushed. "I don't want to mate her. I just think we should adopt her."

Aquos waited for one of the others to ask. When none of them seemed inclined to speak, he figured it was up to him. "What does this word mean, Sally?"

Drake gave him a strange look at his question, but he brushed it off.

"Adoption means we make her our family, even if we aren't related by blood."

"So you feel a debt of honor to my M.J.? Why is this?"

"M.J. stayed and took care of you, when no one else could. She helped my husband's best friend, and a man I happen to really like … I mean you, you dork."

"Not a man," Aquos reminded her, to eager nods from Drake and Luke. "Or a dork." This earned him snorts of disbelief from his friends.

Drake took his wife's hand, "Sally-mine is correct. We will take responsibility for the gir—I mean, woman."

"It is appreciated. This does not change the original question."

"Which is," Aquos asked Luke.

"If she is Omega, she must belong to a clan. Do any of you sense kinship with her?" Aquos and Drake both shook their heads. "Nor I," Luke's grin was barely a quirk of his lips, "though I am sure I would have been told at some point by the other Clan Lords if there were an alternative leader for our group."

Sally took M.J.'s hand in hers. "I don't care where she came from. She's Dragon now."

"Never would I argue with the Queen of the Dragons," Luke gave her a deep bow.

Aquos wanted to argue. *M.J. was his.* Everything within him screamed this truth. He just couldn't do it. Claimed by the dragons, M.J. would have the fiercest warriors at her back. Turbo wouldn't dare to speak her name as long as she was under Drake's protection. With Sally's claim, M.J. now even had a place to go. Not one of the dragon guards on the tesseract would dare to argue with her if M.J. decided to move to the limbo lands.

She had everything as a member of the dragons.

He could offer her nothing but another chance to spend the night tending his failing body, almost drowning.

With a last regretful look at her face, Aquos left M.J., and his heart, behind.

# 21

"Where does he go?"

Sally ignored her husband as she watched Aquos walk silently from the room. His head was so far forward, she feared he'd snap his own neck. From his expression, she was sure he wished he could. "Aquos has some thinking to do," she explained to Drake and Luke.

"I have no idea what to do with this woman," Luke confessed.

"All of you relax. Drake, move M.J. to one of the rooms in our wing. When she wakes up, we'll talk to her about where she's from and what her family is like. Maybe she's like me. A child of someone who is a descendant of one of your Clan Lords. You never know, but we won't find out standing together over her sleeping body, which might make her want to run again."

Drake rested his hand on her belly. "Sally-mine, I know you wish for sisters …"

"I won't decide anything until we speak to her."

He shook off her promise, recognizing she'd already bonded with M.J. "Sally-mine, try to remember, no matter what your choice is here, it is my sworn duty to protect my mate, and the child she grows within her."

"M.J. would never hurt me. I know her."

Drake scowled. "My heart, you not only do not know this woman … you don't even know what she is."

Sally's eyes narrowed. "Try to remember, Drake, I am the Queen of the Dragons, and this woman is now part of our clan."

"I fear, my love, you should remember you just gave Tamar and Hunter leave to join us in our wing as well."

Her heart tripped at this reminder. *Crap. No one told Tamar what to do. Not even the Queen.* Sally did the only thing a woman could do when her husband tried to show her up. She bunted and hoped for the best. "I fear, my heart, you have forgotten there are all of two female dragons left living in the limbo lands. If there is any shot that M.J. is another female, it is our blood sworn responsibility to make every effort to speed her through this transition."

"Yes, my heart." He rested his forehead against hers. "You are correct, of course. But you will not mind when I place your new friend as far from our chamber as possible."

"Of course," she nestled her cheek against his heart. "You're much too noisy to have people close to our bedroom."

The snorts of laughter from Luke did not lessen Drake's enjoyment at his wife's bragging. Sally knew for all he might be noisy when they made love, he made sure his wife was far louder than he.

It was an issue of dragon pride.

 22

M.J. knew she was in a bed. Pillow under her head. Her palms ran over a comforter. Bed. No problem. So the previous night was all some kind of odd, horrible, wonderful, and humiliating dream. Super. She made a mental note not to drink around Squirt for the next ten years or so, hoping to avoid the mortifying possibility of sharing her night's adventures.

Which was when she realized: her face hurt. Her pussy was sore.

And she was definitely missing some basic clothing.

Crap. She sat straight up in the bed, and looked around, eyes bulging.

Double crap. Where the hell was she?

The room she was in looked like it came from one of those fancy magazines she would sneak looks at in the bookstore. The furniture was all gleaming wood with a cherry sheen, the walls were ivory, the bed had damask rose linens. M.J. could recognize the Thomas Kinkade landscapes from her position. And, she feared even more, she was looking at originals.

"Super. I landed in a designer monthly spotlight house."

"No. Just the home for the lost and unwanted."

Looking up, she saw a man who really belonged in a fantasy movie more than in modern day Pennsylvania. He was wearing armor. Really, knight in shining armor. *Crap.* She almost wanted to check that the barbarians weren't about to take a battering ram to the gate. He had salt and pepper hair, dark piercing eyes, and a face that Renaissance artists would use for angels. The way he filled out that armor made her think he had the body those same artists would base warrior kings after. "Hey."

Mr. Armor just gave her one of those looks where the one brow goes up and you see a million things flash in his eyes.

"I'm M.J."

"Yes, Lady M.J., I am known as Ser Tamar." He swept down in a flourishing bow with a rattle of the same said armor. "I am protector of the limbo realm and the foster father for the Queen."

Memories began to click into place for M.J.'s sleep befuddled brain. Sally was the ridiculously hot woman who'd tried to help her last night with goth-boy, and the one the same hot goth-boy had proclaimed a queen. And though she only caught a glimpse of him, her memory also provided the fact that the queen was married to a dude who looked like walking porn. *What the hell was in the water in this place?* The light boy and monster also danced through her mind. She felt like she now knew the complete cast of characters, though wait, wasn't there an …

"Archangel? Did I meet an actual archangel last night?"

Ser Tamar chuckled. "The archangels are regular visitors to this outpost, or so I am told by my men."

"Of course you are."

"Do you have need, Lady M.J.?"

"Why would you care if I did?"

"Queen Salvation chose to 'adopt' you last night. I take it this means something akin to fostering in your world. As far as our clan is concerned, you are now part of the dragonkind."

"I'm a … what now?"

"Dragonkind, my lady. With the Queen choosing you, in our world, your rank is that of the highest noble."

"Seriously?"

"Quite, lady M.J."

"You're not kidding me?"

"I have no sense of humor."

"Really?"

"I assure the queen of just that every time I laugh at her."

"Ah," M.J. nodded. "Good to know."

"I fear, my dear, you are not of the Dragon Clan."

M.J.'s mouth opened and closed twice before her brain accepted and processed the calm statement Ser Tamar made. "This was a question in your mind?"

"The guardian called Gabrielle feels you are one of us."

"What does that mean? One of us?"

"Omega."

"Ser Tamar—"

"You may call me Tamar, Lady M.J."

"Thank you. I'm M.J." She held out her hand to shake, instead, Tamar took it and brushed a kiss on the back of her fingers. M.J. was surprised by how charming it felt. Whenever she read about a guy doing that or saw it in the movies it made her think creepy. *Definitely not that.* 'Oh. Okay. I don't know what the Omega is, but so far I like it."

"We are from a place called Omega. We refer to this planet as Alpha."

"So you're aliens?"

"Omega, my Lady … I mean M.J."

"And on Omega there are dragons?"

Tamar smiled. M.J. suddenly knew that somewhere out there was a very lucky lady. It just wasn't going to be her. "On Omega, you shall find all manners of wondrous beasts. Or at least you would have eons ago. There were dragons and catsu. The Air Clan with the power of the sky, people of the water who command the seas. What's left has so little of that kind. I'm told the ones who are not known have only a single soul left. And of course, I would be grossly amiss if I failed to mention that you have the final progeny of the Light Oracle in this very estate."

"Light Oracle?"

"Something close to your God."

"Well. That's intimidating."

"Nonsense. You are now fostered to the Dragon Clan. There is no clan mightier on either planet. We are the keepers of flame and fire. The guardians of the tesseract. The owners of all that is above and below."

"Even water?"

"No, M.J. Dragons do not control water, though we do tend to hold true affection for it."

Well. That was something. "So because Queen Salvation adopted me, you have no problem considering me part of your … clan?"

"Not one, M.J."

"How come?"

"Queen Salvation has had difficulty accepting her position with dragonkind. Her current pregnancy is making things even more difficult. It is my hope that with your acceptance, she will begin to see the benefits of being our leader, and take her rightful place in the limbo lands."

"And give you time to take a vacation."

"I know not the meaning of this word, but it sounds delightful."

M.J. laughed. "I think I like you, Ser Tamar. I think I like you very much."

"Excellent. Perhaps you will accept my position as your foster father as well. It would make you sister to Queen Salvation."

"I haven't had the best luck with the whole foster system as a rule," M.J. admitted.

"My goal is to change your opinion, Lady M.J."

"Start by not calling me that and we'll do fine."

Tamar chuckled, "Agreed. May I escort you for the day's final meal?"

"I would appreciate it."

"Queen Salvation provided you with a variety of garments to choose from in that room."

"Super." M.J. stood up slowly concerned she was still shaky from the previous night's adventures. "Tell me one thing Tamar, how much does Sally hate it when you insist on calling her Queen Salvation?"

"It vexes her to no end, my lady."

"You and I, Tamar, are destined to get along just fine."

"I would expect no less."

The smile he gave her told M.J. she had definitely just made a real friend. She only hoped she'd be allowed to keep him.

23

Sitting at the table under the stars, Drake couldn't stop scowling. Sally's insistence they have what she liked to call a 'family dinner' wasn't a good idea. There were too many men around his mate. His pregnant mate. He could feel his dragon shift impatiently under his skin. *Think calm, soothing, gentle thoughts*. If his dragon took wing, Sally's beast would respond in kind. The last thing they wanted was for her to transform when the child within was still too precarious.

Luke was at the opposite end of the table, looking wan. Clearly he was still sick, it was a pity the Son of Light refused to admit it. Mach was present, glancing at the empty seat next to him. Drake guessed Turbo would be skipping dinner. Stealth and Blade busily conferred, which occurred frequently lately. On the other side of the table, Hunter stared at his Sally with blatant hunger in his eyes. *Calm, soothing thoughts. Not homicidal ones*. The two empty seats remaining were for M.J. and Tamar, if they ever remembered to show up.

"Are you okay?"

"Of course, love," Drake assured Sally. "I'm just making some mental notes."

"What kind?"

"Basically, that I should ask Hunter to train with me later."

Sally's eyes narrowed as she stared at him. His mate was not a stupid woman. Her mind was one of the first things that had made him fall in love with her. "Since when do you wish to train with Hunter?"

"It will be far easier to kill him that way."

"Drake—"

He cut her off before she could start trying to issue him orders. His woman should know better. She'd issue orders and get upset when he refused to obey, and then he'd have to do what she said anyway. "Fear not, Sally-mine. I am just enjoying the mental exercise of the most effective fashion to end him."

Sally sighed. "Hunter has been a perfect gentleman."

"Hunter is neither gentle nor a man," he brushed a kiss behind her ear. "And he's actively imagining killing me as well, if it gladdens your heart."

"Of course that doesn't gladden my heart," she said with outrage. When she turned to stare daggers at the young dragon, Drake held her chin so she couldn't show just how fiery and sexy her flashing eyes were. "Hunter should know this queen is a one-dragon female. He touches a single hair on your head—"

"Sweet, if he had the skill to touch one hair on my head, I would not be fit enough to serve as your escort."

"Drake—"

"Sally, your M.J. and keeper are arriving."

"My keep—" she scowled at him briefly before jumping to her feet and welcoming Tamar and M.J.

He sat back and watched the night take flight as it would. M.J. took her place at the table, and they tried to treat this like any other meal, just with three additional bodies. Sally's new project was oddly quiet. As was Mach, for that matter. Drake had no idea where Aquos was, but he noticed M.J. kept glancing longingly at the empty chair next to her.

That was interesting.

Stealth and Blade kept conferring softly, basically ignoring the rest of them. Most of the conversation was carried by Sally, Hunter and Tamar, which was not improving his mood. The dragon shifted again, and he could see a ripple of awareness pass under Sally's arm. He had to get away, at least for his family's safety. When he moved to rise from the dinner, M.J. jumped up, muttered a hurried "excuse me" and ran away. The table grew eerily quiet; the only sound was the girl's footsteps fading in the distance.

"Drake?"

One word. The tremulous tone of his mate's voice was all it took. Any concern or jealousy he felt at Hunter's continued interest in his wife dissipated under the heat of his desire to keep everything perfect in the love of his life's world. "Fear not, my heart. I will go and see what ails your adoptee."

Tracking M.J. was not difficult. Dragon senses were normally more sensitive than a human's, but when a pair was going through a quickening as their child grew, they increased exponentially.

He paused in the shadows of the turn of the hall to the great room when he heard M.J. run into Aquos.

"You are well?"

"I am," M.J. responded to him.

"Dinner was not to your liking?"

"Why weren't you there?"

"I ..." It sounded to Drake as if Aquos just swallowed his words—hard.

"You're still healthy, right?"

"I am fine, my, I mean, M.J."

"Then what's wrong? Oh God, don't tell me you were avoiding it because of me, were you?" Drake guessed whatever answer the human woman saw in his best friend's eyes was not to her liking. He caught the sound of a choked off sob, before he heard her fleeing footsteps. At least she was headed back to the room they'd assigned her. Clearly the girl was not acting as a spy or something nefarious. When he stepped into the main chamber for Sanctuary, Aquos had already left.

Continuing, he followed Sally's new project to her chamber.

 24

M.J. wanted to groan in agony when the knock on the door intruded on her misery. *Super.* And here she is, perfectly prepared to face more prying eyes. The tears were running unchecked down her cheeks, along with most of her mascara and liner. Teach her to try and put her girlie on. At least she'd gotten the sobs to stop. *What fresh hell could this be?*

Opening it she realized the answer was … the. Worst. Kind.

Sally's husband was standing on the other side, looking as uncomfortable and miserable as she felt.

"What'd I do wrong?"

He flinched as if she'd hurt him. *As if.* The man was a marble statue come to life, and as big as a freaking skyscraper.

"Pardon?"

"I guess you'd only have followed me if I had done something wrong by leaving dinner. Did I break a rule or is it my turn to clean-up?"

"We have a small army of elementals in this place to handle what you call clean-up, M.J. There has been no breach of etiquette. I swear it." Drake opened the door wider and stepped to the side so the hall sconce light was more on her face. "It seems as if we owe you the apology, however."

"No. Of course not."

Drake lowered his chin and stared at her sternly. M.J. gulped. She had no idea what he was thinking, but she was really hoping it had nothing to do with Aquos. "It's about Aquos," he announced.

Crap. Of course it was. "What about him?"

"What'd he do?"

M.J.'s mouth fell open so wide, Drake used two gentle fingers to close it. "Aquos didn't do anything wrong. I swear it."

"Then why are you so miserable?"

"I … I … please, Drake. It's not something I can discuss."

"M.J., Aquos has been restricted to this estate for years. First due to his looks … and then his illness. His existence has been naught but loneliness and pain. Whatever has gone amiss between the two of you, please, just try talking to him. I swear he is one of the best males in the universe."

"Why do you care?"

Drake smiled as he folded his arms over his chest. "When Aquos met Sally he developed what she called … a crush. You know this, word?" She nodded. "Good. After he developed a bond with my mate, he started to call her Drake's Sally."

"To remind himself she wasn't available."

"Exactly."

"Why are you telling me this?"

"Because, since meeting you, Aquos has started to call my spouse, Sally. You, however, he has named my-M.J. I think my friend has found his other half, and I hate seeing that other half so sad."

"I'm not sure. What I did to him was unforgivable."

Drake snorted. "Aquos would forgive you anything, M.J."

"You don't know—"

"What I know is when I met my Sally I suffered from as many insecurities as she did. Love was what healed us both, and I am quite sure, love will heal you as well, of whatever crime you feel you have perpetrated."

"I'm afraid."

"Funny," he shrugged. "You don't look like a female who is afraid of anything."

"You don't know me. Not really."

"I know you are dragon, now, which makes you my clan."

M.J. smiled, brushing away the tears streaming from her eyes. "No one else has ever wanted me as *clan* before."

"Well, just so you know, when in doubt, we roar and breathe fire, but try talking to Aquos before that. I know my friend, and I am quite sure if you talk to him, you will be pleasantly surprised at the outcome."

 25

Aquos tried not to be jealous. He watched Drake leave M.J.'s room, and he reminded himself that the dragon was his best friend, not to mention married to one of the sweetest, most beautiful, females on this planet. So there was no way he was actually trying to flirt or entice his M.J. Drake had more than enough on his hands with his very pregnant spouse and an entire race of dragons vying for her hand.

Speaking of which, he'd just witnessed from the patio doors, the dragon called Hunter, positively slobbering over M.J.'s beauty. He was going to join the dinner Sally planned when he saw his M.J. spending an evening with her new clan, being given all the due she deserved. So he left, then changed his mind to return to the dinner, only to be intercepted by her in the great room.

He'd decided to track her down to answer the question in his heart that he didn't have the courage to ask after seeing her with Hunter.

But now she was with Drake, and he really didn't know what to think.

Try not to be jealous, he reminded himself. Or at least, try not to let anyone else *know* he was jealous.

He stood outside her door, both fists resting against the wood as he attempted to tamper his rage. He had no right. M.J. might be all he wanted in the world, but maybe she had higher expectations than a dying Water Clan lord.

Besides. She was dragon now. She could have anything she wanted.

However, she was his first. Maybe that trumps dragons? No. Impossible.

Crap. This amazing gift of a woman was driving him stark raving mad.

Just when he was going to leave, the door wrenched open and he stared at the very woman his entire soul called to.

"Hello."

"M.J.," he saw the tears shining on her cheeks. "Did Drake make you cry? I'll kill him. Or better yet, I'll tell Sally he made you cry and she'll do it for both of us. Don't worry about their baby, he won't lack for surrogate fathers."

"No," she smiled at his teasing. "Drake was fine."

"So tell me why? If it was Turbo ..."

"He wouldn't dare," she said. "Not after your threat in the clearing."

"Then why?" Aquos brushed his thumbs over her cheeks. He felt emboldened when she gave a small wistful sigh at his touch, so he cradled her face in his palms. "Whatever it is, I swear I shall banish it."

An elemental carrying a pail of wood logs passed behind them with his head turned away.

"Come inside," she ushered him into her room. "It's more private."

He took a deep breath as he did as she asked. "Why do we need private?"

She winced and he again felt like tracking down whatever or whoever had put the frown in her eyes so he could end them. "Drake was just here. He wanted me to tell you something, well, to talk with you. I thought if we were alone it would go smoother. I'm not sure you understand what happened the other night."

"You saved me."

"I didn't save you, Aquos. I just helped someone in need."

"Tending and saving mean the same thing to my people."

She sighed again, and he knew whatever she was about to tell him was not going to be something that pleased either of them. "Aquos—"

"I don't care."

"What?"

"I don't care about whatever you are trying to tell me." He gently placed his arms around her, feeling his confidence rise when she stepped closer and rested her head against his hearts. "My arms, skin even both of my hearts have hurt since you left my side yester eve. I don't care what Drake said. I don't care what you need to tell me. I don't care about anything, other than you must promise to stay with me."

"Aquos, what happened to us that night ... it wasn't right."

He felt the gorge surge in his throat and he unwrapped his arms. "What do you mean?"

"I took advantage of you."

"What do you mean, my M.J.?"

26

"I raped you, okay?" M.J. threw up her hands in disgust and started to pace back and forth. "You just don't understand. You were half unconscious from your fever, and I just started to maul you. God, I am the worst kind of human being. I make myself sick. You don't know what it's like for women—"

"Do they often go around raping men?"

She frowned at his intrigued expression. *He wasn't getting it. He thought this was a humorous situation.* "No. And not the point, goth-boy. Women have to be so careful once they start getting boobs." The smile that appeared on his face made her want to smack him. *Perfect, M.J. First you rape him and now you abuse him. You are every foster parent you fought against when you were stuck in the system.* "It's dangerous, and you know that, or at least you figure it out pretty fast growing up, if you have any kind of smarts. Then there you are, and you've reached a horribly embarrassing age without ever actually giving in and having sex because you've spent your entire life being on guard against someone taking something you weren't ready to give—"

"M.J.," he held up his hand and she forced herself to stop talking. "My M.J., slow down. Take a breath. Please?"

"Not that many men were anxious to hook up with a girl who looked like I do."

"Your beauty does take my breath, each time I gaze upon you."

Her heart did a flip-floppy thing she was sure was singularly unhealthy, so she glowered. Then she smiled. Then went back to glowering again. He was breaking her brain. Actually breaking her brain. "Aquos …"

"Sweetheart, you are everything beautiful in the universe in one perfect package. How can you not know that?"

"You are the nicest sweetest guy, and I just shouldn't—"

Aquos clasped her shoulders and stared deeply into her eyes. "M.J., I'm not a guy. Please stop thinking of me like that."

"You may be an alien but you're still a guy."

"Male. Not a guy. And it doesn't bother you?"

"That you're a guy?"

"No, M.J." this time it looked like it was he who seemed to have to remind himself to take a breath. "That I'm not from this world."

"Why would it? People from your world probably find you as sexy as I do." He glowed at her muttered compliment, which made her concerned she wasn't communicating well. He wasn't getting the point she was trying to make at all. *Maybe he was still sick?* Oh crap. What if he was still sick and she had to take care of him again? Hopefully, she was just a rapist and not a serial rapist.

"M.J.?"

She realized he must have been repeating her name. He had that bemused and yet impatient expression people often got around her. Then she got lost in the warmth from his eyes, and she couldn't help wondering if she could recreate the curve of his lashes in her next sculpture, when he shook her slightly. He wasn't breaking her brain; it was already screwed up. "What?"

"Finish what you're trying to tell me."

"I did. I think." She mentally reviewed what had actually been said as opposed to the conversation she had in her head and nodded. "I did. I was just trying to explain I raped you, and whatever punishment you feel I should suffer I completely understand. It was wrong, goth-boy. You couldn't consent to anything that happened, and the idea I just proceeded regardless, sickens me to no end."

"Right." He nodded, squeezed her shoulders and stepped away from her. M.J. tightly shut her lids as she waited for him to pass her sentence. "My M.J. ... open your eyes, please."

She did.

Aquos gave her one of those half-smiles that made her heart lurch in response. "Let me get this straight. As best as I can decipher from all the words that just came streaming from your beautiful lips--"

"You shouldn't compliment a rapist."

"What do you think I should do?"

"Throw stuff at me?"

"We'll decide that later. First let me get some things straight. You feel, because I was so sick when we made love—"

"When I raped you."

"This is my turn, my M.J. Please let me speak."

"Sorry."

"You feel because I was so sick when we made love, you raped me."

M.J. nodded.

"And it was your first experience with sex of any kind?"

Her head dropped as the color in her cheeks bloomed. "Yes."

"It is also your belief you are of an embarrassingly advanced age?"

"On our world I am."

"When is the normal age here for joining with a male?"

"I don't know … I think most girls start around sixteen. Well, maybe younger now. Or later, they do tend to spend a lot of time staring at their phones, I'm not sure they actually have the time to glance up and see each other. So let's say fourteen. Crap, I think I'm even more embarrassingly old now."

"How old are you?"

"I'm almost thirty."

"This is in your solar years?"

"What else would it be?" Her head snapped up and when she saw his smug look, she remembered he was from another planet. "Yes, in our years."

"Right."

"How old are you?"

"I, too, am close to thirty."

"Oh," she looked down and sighed.

"Though it would be thirty of our years."

M.J. felt a surge of hope. "They aren't the same?"

"No, my love. They are not."

"Oh God," she looked up with tears in her eyes. "Don't tell me you're younger than me."

"I'm not, love. Never fear that."

"Good. If I was also a pedophile, I'd have to kill myself."

His chuckle at her muttered confession made her want to hit him again. *What the hell is wrong with me?*

"Ok, M.J. This is what we're going to do." Aquos stepped over to the dresser and folded his arms across his chest. "I am going to do to you, exactly what you did to me the other night. Then you are going to tell me if you still feel you raped me, as you keep asserting."

"How would you know?"

"I was fully healed when what happened between us occurred, love."

"But you were so sick."

"And you healed me." He was suddenly in front of her, his palms cupping her face, his thumbs brushing against the corners of her mouth. "When I woke in that hot tub, you were the one who was unconscious.

You fell asleep in the water and I now know you drowned."

"But … how am I alive?"

"I'm a water lord, sweetheart. I commanded the fluid to leave your organs. You opened your eyes and looked at me with all the passion in the universe shining back at me. It took my breath and snatched my heart. Now, do I have your permission to recreate everything and more that happened last night?"

"Yes," she breathed her agreement as her entire body leaned forward.

"Please be sure. Stopping would surely be a tragedy." Aquos cupped the base of her throat. "I'll be focusing on 'the more' tonight if that meets with your approval."

"What do you mean by more?"

"I mean everything the overwhelming force of our passion kept us from experiencing last night."

"Oh," her eyes grew wide as her mouth hung open.

"Say yes again, my M.J."

27

Luke stood outside the tesseract chamber and drew in a deep breath, trying to calm his rioting heart. He had to do it. Gabrielle had been quite clear; he was the only one who could. So, why did he wish with every fiber of his being that it could be someone else who made this call?

Glancing up at the prophecy the elementals had chiseled on the wall years before, he tried to remember how it had felt when they were given this gift. That's what it was meant to be--a gift. He'd never seen it in that manner.

To him, it was always a curse.

From the earliest days of his existence he had known his people were going to destroy their world. Luke had been raised with the burden of the knowledge he would be sent off with the remnants of the clans and their elementals to find the solution to resurrecting their planet. He'd been trained to be a leader. Coached on how to build a new civilization. How to survive far from the crystal palaces of his people, with the technology that made every aspect of their lives easy. Non-stop training for the unenviable day he'd have to live somewhere far from Tian, his beloved homeland, in the place they called the "else."

It wasn't until they'd arrived that he discovered the "else" was known as Earth.

There had been no part of his childhood not dedicated to the responsibility of leading the Omega into tomorrow. He had been drilled on the other clans, how to manage their resources, control people, maintain balance. Lead them into tomorrow. He'd heard that directive so often it became the music of his sleep.

Problem was, leaders were born, not made.

And his biggest shame was he'd never felt like a leader.

He'd barely managed to keep the remaining Clan Lords alive. When they first arrived, with all of the ancient feuds so fresh in their memories, they'd fractured into pieces. It was an act of desperation when this young country took shape in the seventeen hundreds to relocate everyone he could find here.

He'd been forced to leave the rest to the turning pages of time, cast on the winds with no anchor.

Taking another deep breath, he stepped into the portal chamber. When they built Sanctuary over this room, they'd decided their most important council meetings would be held inside. No more would they maintain the illusion of singular ruling. They had to stand together. The elementals had labored to create them thrones to use when in conference, trying to make them feel comfortable by recreating that which they loved best. His was made from a crystal they found deep inside the heat of the world. Clear columns of glass-like substance, reflecting the blue and silver light of the portal into a million shards to illuminate the room.

It didn't come close to dispelling the darkness inside him.

The two dragon knights came to attention upon his entering. Both were dressed in the silver plate of a bygone age, the one with dark hair was familiar. The red-head he'd never seen before. Where were Tamar and Hunter? It was usually their job to stand watch. He nodded at the two knights. "Forgive my intrusion. I'll need a moment alone, please." They shared a look of unease, but silently quit the room. When the door was shut behind them, Luke moved in front of the tesseract.

Kneeling, he placed his hands palm up on his thighs, and he tried another deep breath. "Oracle, I beseech you, come to me."

Nothing.

Closing his eyes, he tried to imagine his mother, the last time they met. Her long white hair, braided with small spring flowers growing from the folds, the sweep of her gown, the color of a night's sky scattered with stars. He never once remembered her touching him. Or even smiling at him.

Hugs and cookies were never going to be in the Oracle's inventory.

Right now, all he needed was for her to answer his call.

"Oracle, our need is great. I beg of you to heed my cry. Your children falter in their task. Please respond."

Still nothing.

He sighed. *It couldn't be easy, could it?* Nothing with his mother ever was. Screw that. Nothing in his eternally cursed life had ever been close to easy. Or simple. Or pleasant. Forget peaceful or loving.

If the head wearing the crown was heavy, the ass in the throne of light was fucking tortured.

"Oracle, damn it, just answer me already."

Why would he possibly think yelling and cursing would inspire her?

Rising, he began to pace in front of the churning light as he remembered the last time he'd received direction from beyond the veil. It had been after the human's world war, and he'd wanted to move them to a secluded island off the coast of New Zealand. He'd tired of this place and was worried about the Americans' growing paranoia over the rising tide of Communism.

Somehow, he thought their discovering aliens in their midst would seem like a worse threat.

They had started the ritual to move the portal when the Oracle appeared. Two words. All she gave them. "You stay." With that, and a puff of smoke, because Mom did have a flair for the dramatic, she disappeared.

Now when he needed her most, she wasn't responding.

Fuck this. If she wouldn't talk to him, he'd make her appear and finally give him some bloody answers.

Luke turned onto the portal and thrust his hand into the light.

Screaming with agony, the searing hideous pain sent him flying into the far wall. He panted as his vision filled with stars and a slick sweat covered his entire body. Swallowing swiftly, he managed to keep his stomach from evacuating through his mouth. He stared at the bone-deep burns on his arm with shock. *What in the seven rings of hell was that?*

"Only a creature of the Light may enter."

Turning to Gabrielle, he looked between the tesseract and his burned, useless arm, confused. "I am the Son of Light."

"You were, Luke. One must wonder what you are now, though."

"This is why she won't answer me?"

Gabrielle moved closer, and waved her hand over his burned arm. It didn't heal him, but it did lessen some of the pain to a manageable level. "Hardest thing for a parent to face is the moment they no longer recognize the child they bore. The Oracle lives, Luke. I am not as sure of your Mother."

"I can't do it, Gabrielle. I'm useless for them."

"Quitting is not in your make-up, Luke."

"How would you know?" He rubbed his undamaged hand over his face as he rose. "How would I? I have no fucking idea who I am anymore."

"You are Luke, Lord to the Light Clan."

"That title sucks." Luke moved to collapse on his throne, but decided leaning against the wall was safer, not to mention closer. "I have never understood what in the seven rings of hell it meant, Gabrielle."

"You are also brother, friend, and champion."

"I don't think anyone else thinks that but you."

She didn't answer. She was just gone with a regretful shrug. Luke wanted to curse, but figured he'd pretty much pushed it as far as he should for one day's time with the powerful women in his life. He chose instead to make his slow, plodding way back to his rooms where he could lick his painful wounds in peace.

28

Aquos waited. It felt like it took an eternity. M.J.'s brown eyes shone from the trace of tears still clinging to their surface. Behind her gaze, Aquos could see a million thoughts rolling around. Her skin was like milk chocolate, yet with a faint flush, casting a fetching pink into her cheeks. This was what attracted him to her: there was so much going on beneath her surface. Her lips as red as strawberries, parted slightly as she took a deep breath in preparation of an answer.

Thank the Oracle. She was finally going to respond.

"Yes. A million times yes."

Aquos took a moment to let out his breath and smile. His woman just gave him complete freedom to do everything he ever dreamt of with her. Actually, technically, to him, his M.J. just declared herself his woman for the first time. And he couldn't be happier.

"Excellent answer, my M.J." His fingers speared into her brandy colored hair, he tilted her head back, and his mouth covered hers. This was no gentle tasting. This kiss was meant to brand his taste and touch into the fiber of her being. Her mouth fell open at a brush of his tongue and they were dueling, inside each other; he used his tongue in long slow strokes, determined to give her a tease of all that was to come.

And he was determined to deliver.

M.J. seemed to like her preview. She stepped closer to him, pressing her body against his, her hips circling against his pelvis. He tilted his legs so that her movements would rub against his cock and he was able to hit her clit.

He could feel her. Every inch of her, inside and out, the water in her body giving him an epic list of signals of how she was responding to his actions.

And the biggest sign he noticed was just how wet she was.

His lips fused to hers, Aquos kept one hand in her hair, angling her head to continue to make this kiss last as long as he hadwaited for a woman like this to come into his life. The other slid over the small of her back, to the curve of her ass. He took a moment to squeeze one cheek, appreciating the sheer, elegant muscled form of her body. One he fully intended to taste every inch of.

Again, he took the moment to appreciate the resilience of her ass, before he slid his hand down lower so he could wrap it around her upper thigh and use the leverage to lift her onto the bed.

He managed to follow her without once losing connection with her lips.

Keeping their mouths fused felt like it would maintain the balance of the galaxy.

M.J.'s body softened under his frame, cradling him. His hands traveled down, ripping her shirt apart. When he cupped her breasts, she arched her back to thrust them more firmly into his hold. His lips began to travel over her cheek, savoring the curve of her neck, nibbling lightly on the rampaging pulse beneath his kisses.

When he got to her bra it took little more than a flick of his wrist to get it separated. Her breasts were small, but he could see her nipples pebble at the mere brush of his breath across their tips. She was so responsive to him. Aquos felt his cock swell to a painful level. He'd always wanted a woman like this, but he never imagined she'd be a creature of such sheer and utter perfection.

Her legs traveled up his sides to belt his waist. M.J. kept her hips moving, not used to how to angle her movements so that his straining erection would rub against her clit and give her some relief. Aquos reminded himself to slow down. He was determined to make this take as long as possible.

It was definitely the more he was looking forward to the most.

29

M.J. was so frustrated she wanted to hit the beautiful man setting her body on fire. Wrenching her lips from his kiss, she managed to gasp out her command, "Aquos ... you're taking too long."

"We're going to take all night, my love. If I had my way, we'd take an eternity." He cupped her face to look deeply into her eyes. She whimpered in protest when he shifted his hips away from her boiling-over softness. "There will never be enough time for me to properly worship you."

She pushed him over, quickly following so he'd stay that way, and sat on her heels on either side of him. Aquos folded his arms beneath his head, and gave her one of his special, knee melting, half-flirty smiles. He knew what he was doing. She tried not to think about sitting on top of him, her bra and shirt off, her pants unsnapped, just waiting for him to finish the job. He lifted one eyebrow as he waited for her to decide. M.J. tried to think of some way to torture him as much as she felt the pain of denial. She shifted her hips as a flood of moisture coated her center in response. His dark eyes were warmed with passion and ... approval. M.J. couldn't imagine anything being more sexy. Trying to make her voice as deep and growly as he did, she informed him, "I don't want to be worshipped, goth-boy."

"Tell me what you do want, my M.J."

"You," leaning down M.J. brushed kisses along the line of his jaw to his neck. His skin was stubbled, yet still soft against her lips. His hands opened and closed on her hips, though he made no effort to control or push her. "I want you on top of me. Underneath me. Every position that is possible, please. I need you inside me, goth-boy. What do I need to do to convince you? I may not have the experience, but I have done research. Loads of it."

His chuckles at her confession made her punch him lightly in the side. She moved to dismount from him, but his hands on her hips held her in place. "I am not laughing at you, love."

"Then what was so funny?"

His eyes caressed her face, lingering on the tears held back by her lashes. "I was laughing with the joy you give me, M.J. I would never make fun of you. I would never make you feel less than you are."

"I don't understand you."

"What do you mean?"

"How can you possibly be real? I keep thinking you're some kind of hallucination my lonely heart created."

"I am quite real, M.J." His hands banded against her back and she was flipped so that she had a hot, sensual man blanketing her who was clearly determined to discover every aspect of her body she would allow. "Let me prove it."

M.J. groaned as her entire body felt like it was trying to melt into him. "How many times do you want me to say yes, goth-boy?"

"Say yes for the rest of your life and I may feel confident, but I doubt it."

"I don't understand you" she softly repeated.

"Then stop thinking," he ordered. "And start feeling." Aquos licked her lower lip, making her crane up more, trying to force one of his deep kisses. Instead he moved his wicked lips to her throat, nibbling on her rioting pulse. He nipped her shoulder, smoothing the sting with his raspy tongue. M.J. tried to spear her fingers into his hair so she could drag him back to her lips, but he caught her hands in his and squeezed. Wrapping them around the filigree in the headboard, he gave her a mock glower, "Keep them there."

"What about ..."

"Remember, my M.J., this is my turn to take advantage of you. Now do as I say."

Her teeth started to bite at her lower lip, prompting Aquos to separate them with a brush of his fingers. "I'm the only one who gets to bite you, understand?" she gave him a tentative nod, which earned her a long lick up her neck to her ear, where he nibbled on the lobe. "I promise you'll like it when I do."

"Okay," she whimpered when he nipped her ear again.

His lips continued on their path, moving down her neck to the swell of her breast. Her nipples throbbed with longing, hoping he'd touch them, or even suckle, M.J. wasn't sure anymore, she just wanted something to happen. Something that would ease the relentless throbbing in her breasts, her core, her everything. His tongue traced around her aureole, as her breathing increased. Her feet rubbed against the sheets, her hips kept trying to tilt so she could rub her pulsing clit against something.

When Aquos finally wrapped his lips around her nipple and sucked, it immediately triggered her orgasm and made her give a small scream as something tight within her suddenly broke apart.

Only to snap back together even tighter.

"Oh sweetheart," his hand covered the tip of her aching, abandoned breast, as his words sent soft puffs of air against her hyper sensitive skin, "you were so ready for this, weren't you? It's okay, we've got miles to go, yet."

"Miles? Miles?" she screeched. "Are you calling me fat?"

He chuckled with his lips against the underside of her breast so she could feel it resonate throughout her core. "I would know your soul no matter what size your form, sweet. But for the record, to me you are perfect."

"No one is perfect."

"You are." This time his lips wrapped around her abandoned nipple while his other hand covered her other breast and squeezed rhythmically. While she was rubbing against him like a cat in the height of heat, he moved away and started traveling down. *Finally*, she thought to herself. Oral sex sounded embarrassing and messy, but right now she'd do anything to make the unbearable ache beating like a drum from between her legs just go away.

Aquos used his eyelashes against her ribs to make her giggle at the flutters. He circled her belly button with his tongue, and then moved lower, placing brief kisses in a straight line above her pants. "I think it's about time we took these off, huh?"

"Here I thought you were going to try and leave them on."

"Nope," he smiled at her, before wrenching her pants and underwear off in one motion.

M.J. squealed with surprise, covering her pussy with both hands. "Goth-boy!"

"You wanted them off." His tone said innocence but his look was pure devil.

"Not like that."

He began to alternate kisses down the fronts of her legs. "Are you sure, my M.J.?" His teeth nibbled the arch of her foot before he licked her toes, causing her to start giggling. "Somebody's ticklish."

"No, I'm not."

"You sure?"

This time he sucked her entire big toe into the warm cavern of his mouth, setting off a fresh round of laughter. "Not ticklish, goth-boy. It's just that I never heard of anyone wanting to suck someone's toes before."

"Not even in all your research?"

She froze as she stared down her body into his eyes. The warmth she saw there, heated her body more than any heater ever could. "No, goth-boy, I never saw it in any of my research."

"Good," he nipped her little toe. "I wish to claim as many of your firsts as I can."

"You can have them all, goth-boy. You're the only one I've ever met I wanted to give them to."

He purred. He actually purred with satisfaction at her vehement confession. "My M.J." Two words. Spoken so softly, she almost didn't hear him. M.J. was going to ask him for more words, whole sentences even. But then he started to lick slowly up the inside of her leg, and she found she had no ability to do more than softly pant her need.

She clenched at the filigree iron in her hands, trying to use the bite of the metal in her flesh as a way to keep from flying apart. Her hips started to arch up, as if he was already on top of her.

Then his thumbs gently separated her dripping folds. His breath ran over her aching core. She gasped with need, no longer caring about what she sounded like or what he would think. She needed him. She needed him now inside her. M.J.'s grip on her headboard tightened and she used that hold to leverage her hips upward when he licked her. He actually ran his tongue from where she was dripping the most, straight to her clit. Then she wrapped his lips around that nubbin of flesh and he suckled it, too.

She couldn't take anymore.

M.J. speared her fingers into his hair and dragged at Aquos until she could wrench him down for her kiss. She tasted herself on his mouth, and it wasn't gross like she'd thought it would be. "Get inside me, goth-boy. Or I promise you, I will rape you again, and not feel even the slightest bit guilty."

"There's my girl." He slid one hand beneath her ass, lifted her hips and then she felt it. His dick was long and hard, hot as sin, and her entire body felt like it blossomed open for him. He slid inside her in one smooth glide, and she arched again into his advance, as a small cry escaped her lips. He froze. His body locked in place, his muscles carved out beneath his skin in intricate detail. She squirmed beneath him, and he growled. "Just making sure you're okay, sweetheart." When she eagerly nodded he chuckled. "I guess we can finish."

"It's about damn time," she retorted.

Aquos began to thrust and she panted. Each time he filled her, small grunts escaped her lips. His cock was so long, it felt like it was filling every part of her to overflowing, its warm pulsing causing a whole new level of sensations for her eager body to absorb.

When he went faster, his eyes blazed at her and she swore she could see the entire universe reflected back in their starry depths, just before all the stars ever created suddenly exploded within her.

* * *

Aquos followed her over when M.J. screamed out her release. He rested his sweaty face against her cheek as she continued to regain control of her breathing. Her earlobe was right there, so he gave it another nibble, before pressing a light kiss to her cheek. "You are amazing."

She closed her eyes and groaned as he withdrew from her body. "You are, too. I finally understand why people make such a big deal about sex."

"Not sex, my M.J. This was making love."

M.J. speared her fingers in his hair, rubbing his scalp, enjoying the feel of the silky strands of his hair against her skin. "Got it. Making love."

"And it was never, and could never be, rape."

Her cheeks flooded with blood and she groaned. "I'm an idiot."

"You, my heart, are adorable. An idiot you are not."

"Thank you, goth-boy."

He kissed her, because she was lying beneath him, still looking like a pin up girl, with hair tousled from his fingers, eyes large and full of wonder, lips swollen from his kisses, and skin covered with burns from his stubble. She was everything he'd ever dreamt of having, and everything he knew he could never deserve.

He kept kissing her because she was running her hands over his head and back, as if she was filled with as much wonder as he was.

When he settled beside her, he smiled as she rolled into his embrace, knowing this was where she belonged for the rest of time. Her head on his chest, her hand on his shoulder, even her leg was bent over his thighs. He wrapped his fingers around her calf, and kept running his thumb over her satiny, caramel skin. "Tell me about your life outside."

"You mean my home?"

"Home? You have such a thing?"

"Squirt. I have Squirt."

Aquos chuckled, "I have no idea what a squirt is."

"Squirt is my foster sibling. I didn't have a home before I met Squirt's Mom. She treated me well. Like an equal. When Squirt's Mom died, I thought I'd be on my own for all time. But Squirt wouldn't leave me, and turned away every other person who tried to separate us. Loyalty is a heady thing when you don't have any previous experience with it, and Squirt has always given it to me freely."

"This I understand."

"What's having a home like for you?"

"I have never had a home before I met you." When she craned up to stare at him with her mouth hanging open in surprise, he shrugged and partially closed his eyes to avoid her piercing stare. "This place, Sanctuary, these men, even this planet. None have been my home. My home is with you now, my M.J. I will have no other. I need no more."

"Aquos—"

He pressed two fingers against her lips to stop her from saying anything that might lessen the importance of the moment. He knew this world, and the way this time worked. Guys like him were not considered sane. "I'm not looking for you to respond, my M.J. I am only giving you the honesty you deserve."

"I still can't believe you're real."

"Well," he reached up and snatched his cell phone from the bedside table. "I cannot believe that I have neglected to offer you the use of a phone. I appreciate you staying here while we figure everything out, but you probably would like to call your Squirt and assure them of your good health."

"Thank you." She dialed a number into the phone and held it to her ear, her eyes nervously flickering between him and the far side of the room. Aquos wondered what she saw when she looked around. This suite was decorated as much of the mansion was, with heavy dark wood furniture, pastoral landscapes, and soothing neutral colors. He knew that some of the Clan Lords had personalized their suites over the years, but this was one of the many guest rooms that had stood idle since they built Sanctuary in the late seventeen hundreds. There was an entire wing the elementals insisted they needed that no one even bothered to set foot in.

He hoped she wasn't so happy in this particular suite she'd be resistant to moving to his wing rather than the dragons.

After she left a message for her Squirt, along with the phone number, she hung up, and returned it to the bedside table. Settling back in his embrace, she sighed. Then she started to move her leg against his thigh, and part of him instantly began to elongate in response. "My M.J. ... what are you doing?"

"Thinking."

"About what," his hand slid over her thigh and straight to her core to cup her heat against his callused palm.

"I believe you mentioned something about more?"

He chuckled as he moved her to lie on top of him so he could properly appreciate the curve of her ass, not to mention the beautiful blanket she made. "I did mention more, so much more. I take it you are ready for another episode?"

"Definitely," she smiled as she leaned down to kiss him with all the longing and need in her body.

 30

A soft knock on the door was the only thing that could entice Aquos from his position wrapped around M.J. He frowned when he saw Luke on the other side. Rubbing a hand over his face, he asked, "What now?"

"I'm sorry, dude."

"Please tell me we aren't being attacked by mercs again."

"Nah, but we need to see your human."

"I thought Gabrielle established she's anything but."

"Still need to converse with her."

"How come?"

Luke sighed, his face contorting with pain. "There are some questions, A. Questions only she can answer."

"Aw, shit, Luke. Now? Really? We were up late last night."

"We'll get you guys fed and through this as fast as possible so you can go back to what you were doing. Best I can offer."

"Right. And by offer, you mean command."

"I don't do it often, Aquos. So when I do, you damn well better respond. We clear?"

Aquos slammed the door, hoping Luke was having another migraine and the noise would fuck his Luke's shit up. He tried to prepare himself to tell M.J. they were being called out, when he saw she was awake. And staring at him with eyes so big they felt like they were swallowing him whole. "Problem?"

"Luke says he needs to see us and get some answers."

M.J. shuddered and he wanted to track down his fearless, so-called, leader and beat the crap out of him. "Where I'm from that kind of sentence usually ended with my getting kicked out on my ass."

"No one," he strode to the bed and grasped her upper arms, "no one is kicking any part of you."

"I don't know what kind of rodeo you guys are running here, goth-boy, but clearly Luke's the one holding the reins. The head-angel-face-in-charge. If he wants me gone, I'm getting gone."

Aquos leaned forward to cover her beautiful mouth with his and remind her of everything they were together. "Luke wants you gone, my M.J., I'm going with you. Now angel-face did promise us some food, so let's go and get fed, deal with whatever nonsense the Omegicon demand, and come right back here."

"Really?" she wrapped her arms around his neck and arched into his body as he ran kisses down her face. "Why would we do that?"

"I have at least a hundred other ways I plan on proving to you the other night was no rape." He laughed at her irritated expression. Pulling her from the bed as he rose, he pointed to the sunlight streaming through the windows. "And then there's always the pond. I have a whole different set of abilities I can't wait to see how much pleasure it gives you, my M.J."

"Pond?" she locked her muscles to slow him down. "I don't swim, Aquos."

"Really?"

"Born and raised in the foster care system. No one ever bothered to teach me, and I always lived in the city, so there was no place to learn."

His hands wrapped around her hips and he pulled her into the curve of his body so he could enjoy every inch of her softness melting around him. "Trust me, my M.J. The last thing you ever have to fear is the water. Now, let me get this Omega nonsense out of our way so we can go back to what's important."

"I've created a monster," she giggled.

"You have no idea."

Aquos kept his concern from her. *Why was Luke demanding this audience now?* Gabrielle had to be wrong about M.J. She was human, she must just be special. He could tell she was special just by looking at her, why couldn't the archangel? Gentle teasing and loads of long kisses kept M.J. from sensing his unease. When they made it to the great room for the building and he didn't see any of the other Clan Lords, he realized this might be more serious than he realized.

"Everything ok?"

"Luke didn't tell me where he wanted to meet," he confessed. Spotting an elemental passing by, he called out to her, "Excuse me." The girl in the red robes stopped and turned slowly. When she saw the pair of them, she dropped to her knees, leaning forward until her forehead was pressed against the ground. *What the hell?* Elementals don't bow. At least they never have to him, and he didn't remember seeing any mention of it in the historic rolls Luke kept. He was confused. "Okay. Uhm, Tana, isn't it? Forgive me, I've been so sick lately I haven't gotten everyone's names right. Sally just told us we had to start to learn."

"Good for her," M.J. muttered.

The girl just knelt there, quivering so much, waves were visible in the drape of the fabric of her robes.

"Aquos, do you normally make them do this? Because I am really not down with the slave shit. Do you know the history of this country?" He gave her a funny look as he tried to verbalize the fact that he witnessed it firsthand. She was standing on a spot, he was pretty sure, where George Washington once threw up. "Tell me you don't make the elementals treat you guys like some kind of medieval gods."

The medieval gods weren't nearly as bad as the Egyptian ones. He probably shouldn't tell her that either. He shook his head, "I have no idea why she's doing this."

"Well, tell her to stop."

Tana immediately jumped to her feet. She moved so fast she was reeling a little. Aquos opened and closed his mouth a few times as he tried to figure out what he was seeing. "I need to know where the Clan Lords are meeting."

She didn't answer. Aquos was still dealing with the shock of an elemental acting so out of character. They were usually ghosts who were incredibly efficient and dedicated. None of them had ever asked any of the elemental classes to behave with such obedience.

"He won't bite," M.J. promised the girl. "I promise. You can answer."

"In the tesseract chamber, my lord."

"Thank you."

"My name is M.J.," she held out her hand to the elemental who stared at it as if it was going to bite her. "It's nice to meet you, Tana."

The girl fell to her knees again with her head smack against the floor. *What in the name of the Oracle was going on?* Aquos braided his fingers with M.J.'s and tugged her to get them moving again. The elementals could be figured out later. First there was whatever bullshit Luke was about to throw at him.

After that they could figure out who the hell had broken the elementals.

31

M.J. knew something was wrong with goth-boy. She just couldn't tell what it was. He had clearly been nervous since angel face had banged on the door. Then whatever his servant had done had really pushed her guy over the edge. His eyes were narrowed, he kept looking over his shoulder down the hall from where they came and back down at his feet as if there were some answers to be found in the polished wood floors.

What the hell was going on in this place? Who knew rural Pennsylvania could be so interesting.

Aquos paused outside a set of double doors that appeared to be burnished metal. Like vault doors in a bank. Only bigger with fancy carving all over the surface. *This is interesting.* M.J. reached out a hand to touch one of the more intricate motifs when Aquos caught her. "Careful, sometimes the elementals treat these types of things with poison to prevent anyone from sabotaging them."

Super. *Don't touch the pretty artwork.* Got it.

He still seemed to be weighing something, staring at the door. She glanced around, trying to figure out if there was some way she could help him. On the opposite wall was a chiseled poem with beautiful calligraphy on it. She couldn't make out the language, but the words were so intricately designed on the piece, it was a different kind of art. That was the thing about being an artist, she tried to find beauty in everything she saw. It was Squirt's mom who'd taught her that through looking for the beauty she could find truth.

"Aquos, what is that?"

"Our prophecy."

"Your what, now?"

"It was the set of instructions we were given before coming to this planet. A command from our Oracle on how we could save our world."

Oh. Of course it was. She rolled her eyes.

He was lucky he was so damn hot. And nice. And sweet. Not to mention really amazing in bed. Any sane woman would have run for her life.

Which was when he wrenched open the door and ushered her inside.

They were so not in Kansas anymore.

* * *

The Architect stood on the rise above the mansion, trying to see how his plan was continuing. He didn't understand what was wrong. The poison should have taken the Water Clan lord out. With Aquos gone, the other lords would follow with ease. How they could not realize that Aquos was the one who kept their organs and blood balanced was beyond him.

He also didn't comprehend where the elementals had gone. Controlling them was one of the best decisions he had made, and a coveted power he had honed from the most ancient scrolls in the library. Suddenly they were refusing to heed his orders, and no longer even responded to his calls.

The only good news was the poison worked on the scouts. They'd be gone soon enough.

Poison was another of the skills his years of research gifted him.

Research was something the other lords taunted him about.

All the knowledge of centuries, wasted on a group of males who never understood that you cannot build a strong future without understanding your past. The answers they sought were always in the books.

The elementals still did not respond to his mental call, and he cursed.

How did he lose control?

And when would he get it back?

32

Luke was seated in his crystal throne when Aquos and M.J. finally decided to join them. He'd managed to get everyone in the chamber at the same time, for once. Only the two who most needed to attend were late. Not that he could blame the Water Clan lord. If Luke had found his woman, he'd have just blown off something as banal as Clan Lord business so he could enjoy his love at leisure.

Mach was there alone because Luke demanded only one member of the Speed Clan show. It wasn't like Turbo had made any points with Aquos or M.J., for that matter. Stealth, Blade and Drake were all there. Though Drake had insisted Sally also be present, so she was seated on Drake's lap. Luke knew that Altea of the Mage Clan was inside the room, but he'd never deign to show himself for something as common as identifying to which clan a lost member of their race belonged.

So the Mage throne stood empty, with every shadow and pocket of darkness feeling as if it had eyes. *Judging him.*

The dragons also had two knights guarding the tesseract, as was their ancestral right. Luke didn't recognize these two, and he wondered where Tamar and Hunter had disappeared to. By all accounts, both the dragon knights were fitting in nicely with their little band of refugees. They'd already managed to kick most of the others off the high score lists on their favorite video games.

"Let's get whatever this is over with."

"I don't see why we have to do this at all," Sally said. "The Dragon Clan has already claimed M.J."

Luke smiled when he noticed Sally's words made the two dragon knights immediately come to attention, and send interested smiles in M.J.'s direction. She just slipped behind Aquos and ignored them. *Good for her.* Nothing like a loyal female. Not that he'd know. The only female he'd been interested in for ages had disappeared and he still had no idea where she'd gone.

Or even what her name was.

"Right. Sally—"

"Queen Salvation."

Luke's eyebrows felt like they were trying to escape his face, they went up so high. "Seriously, Drake? You're shoving formalities down my throat right now? You think I need this shit?"

"Her title is more than a formality, as much as she tries to ignore it. If you're going to drag Aquos and his lady into this mock court, I'm damned well going to insure my mate is given proper respect. Sally is named the salvation of our people, and the one who resurrected our entire race. Don't fuck with me on this, Luke. Not to mention, M.J. has been named dragon, so she deserves my protection."

Sally patted her male. "Sweetheart, I'm sure Luke didn't mean anything. You're just tense because of the closed space."

"I'm tense because Luke dragged us all out of bed—"

"Only the ones with a female," Mach muttered.

"Enough," Luke roared, jumping to his feet. "I appreciate that Queen Salvation," he paused so he could glance at Drake, who gave him a curt nod. "Declared M.J. a dragon, but that doesn't alter the question we all have."

"Care to clue me in here, angel face?"

He winced as most of the men, even Sally and the two dragon knights, laughed heartily at the human's nickname for him. Or not human. Crap, he couldn't even keep this shit straight anymore. He counted to ten while everyone got the laughter out of their systems. *Bunch of fucking hyenas.* "You know we are not of this world. According to one of your kind's guardians, you are not either. So the question, M.J., is what the fuck are you?"

"I have no idea." M.J. started to back-up as if they were attacking her. Luke realized that was probably exactly what it felt like. Aquos adjusted his hold by wrapping his body around her. "No one ever told me anything about my family. I've always been M.J. Storm. I don't know more than that."

"She was raised in something called foster care."

"Oh, M.J.," Sally said. "I am so sorry."

"Sally, be quiet."

Drake growled in response to Luke's rebuke.

"Look, I was one of the lucky ones. Eventually I landed with Squirt's mom and she was great. But I have no idea who my family was."

"I am," Aquos cupped her face so she would look in his eyes.

"Yes, goth-boy, and I love that you think that. But Luke seems really caught up on my last name or something." She turned to Luke and leaned back against Aquos when he stood behind her and belted his arms around her waist. "I don't think I can do what goth-boy does. I've never been a big fan of water."

"Bet you are now."

Everyone laughed at Mach's drawled observation, M.J. even blushed.

Luke felt the pain surge in his head and his stomach turned. "Does anyone else sense any form of kinship with her?"

No one spoke.

"Are you all sure? I know she isn't of my kind, but I have no clue who she belongs to."

"Me. She belongs with me," Aquos said.

"The scouts are not here."

Altea chose to bless them with his fucking presence by forming from the shadows in the far corner. The dragon knights softly swore and stepped closer to the kaleidoscope light show that was the tesseract in the center of the chamber. Luke couldn't figure out why, unless they were considering jumping through it to return to the limbo lands. The Mage were part of the key ingredient to open the tesseract in the first place. It was one of the many reasons why Altea despised Drake. When he agreed to open the portal so the Clan Lords could flee for their lives, the Mage were sacrificed against their will.

"Welcome, Mage Clan Lord. Do you know where Keva is?"

"The scouts are fracturing, Son of Light."

Luke took a deep breath as he tried to understand what the elusive clan leader was saying. He glanced at Stealth, hoping the Air Clan would step in and help. Stealth was busy staring at M.J. with something akin to puzzlement? He hoped so. Maybe it meant Stealth sensed something. Other than that, they had zero to work with. "Is there something we can do to help them?"

"Fractures for their kind are permanent. Even you will be unable to piece them back together again. No matter. Their fates were made generations ago," Altea shrugged. "It's of no consequence."

"Do you know who this female belongs to?"

"It is clear."

Luke closed his eyes as he prayed for patience. "Perhaps you'd care to share?"

"The female is the Water Clan's now."

"Damn straight," Aquos said.

"I don't mean who she's sleeping with!" Luke roared.

"The dragon bitch—"

Drake jumped to his feet, snarling. The two dragon knights pulled their swords with equal rancor contorting their faces.

"You will not violate Sanctuary," Luke jumped to his feet and almost went to his knees as the pain hit him like a dropped building. "Not by deed, or word." Sally rushed to the dragon knights and got them to put away their swords. Drake stayed on alert, staring at Altea, with a lifetime of hate in his eyes. *Fuck that.* Drake had thousands of years of hate in his eyes. "Apologize Mage, or by the Oracle's word, I will put you in the ground myself."

"I apologize," Altea slithered to the entrance of the chamber and stared back at them with eyes the glowed with the fire of the universe. "Though soon enough, there will be no Light Clan to demand such obedience."

When the mage quit the chamber, Luke allowed his body to collapse back into the throne. Sally calmed Drake, and the others just watched him with wary eyes. "I guess there is more for us to discuss than M.J.'s heritage. My apologies. Whatever balance Sally's arrival brought seems to have skipped me. I fear there is something still making me sick."

Blade's fingers reached for his sword. "Why did you not say?"

"I was ashamed to be so weak."

"You realize the mage just threatened your life," Drake said.

"No, dragon. No dragon-mage feud now, please. Altea was just referring to this illness I suffer from."

"This illness has affected all of us in different ways, Luke. You are no different." Mach sat forward. "We'll find a way to help you."

"Your sentiment is kind, Mach. But let's be honest. You can't even figure out what's wrong with Turbo. Speaking of which … we're going to have to talk about him as well. His anger is out of control. I don't have proof, but I think he's going through transpotheosis." When he caught Sally opening her mouth to speak he held up a hand. "Turbo is changing into his true form, a catsu. Sort of like Drake and you when you transform into your dragon selves. The difference is the dragon maintains their higher mental functions. Catsu are creatures of the wild."

"They know killing, eating and dying."

"And nothing else," Luke finished for Mach.

"I care nothing about Turbo since he hurt M.J."

"No." Her one word was enough to have every person's eyes fly to M.J., and Aquos whirl around with surprise. "He was your friend once, goth-boy. We don't abandon people who have cared about us."

"He hurt you," Aquos brushed two fingers across the cheek Turbo had hit.

"True. But he was your friend. You called him brother. I take that kind of thing really seriously. And from what they're saying, he's not exactly in control of himself right now. He was a dick to me in the forest, but I don't believe he meant to strike me the second time." She looked at Luke and tilted her head. "Is it possible that whatever is wrong with you is also effecting the monster?"

"You call my cousin the monster?"

M.J.'s nod to Mach's question made his head drop with shame.

"Got a problem with that?"

He shrugged at Aquos's question. "Nah. I was just … surprised."

"You mean ashamed, don't you?"

The eyes he turned to M.J. and Aquos were haunted with pain. "Turbo is more than a cousin; he really is a brother. We joke around and shit. But we love women. I can't believe he hurt you, M.J. I am so sorry for it." He strode across the room to kneel before her. "If you wish to declare recompense I will gladly serve it for him. The Speed Clan is in your—"

"Stop." M.J. grabbed a piece of his shirt and pulled him up from the floor. "Please stop. All these people kneeling at my feet are making me nervous." She held out a hand to Mach, "How about we shake and be friends?"

Mach jumped up and down and shook his whole body, sending M.J. and Sally into a round of giggles that made all the men in the room smile. Mach winked at M.J. before boasting to the men, "Works every time, my brothers." Turning back to the female whom his clan had wronged, he repeated his vow. "If there is anything I can do for you, M.J., I do so gladly. I don't know what's going on with T, but I swear this is not who he is or what we're about."

"I'll take your word for it."

"Hold up," Luke leaned forward, rubbing hard at his throbbing forehead. "What do you mean about people kneeling at your feet?"

"No one wants to hear what Aquos does with her in bed," Blade said.

"I guess this is the time for us to talk about the elementals."

33

Drake scowled as Sally picked up a barbecued rib and ripped into it with her teeth. "See, honey? I'm eating. Eating meat. Isn't that great?"

He had to force the smile back from breaking past his glower. They were seated outside, near the grill, enjoying a feast that had been assembled while they were in council. He could say one thing for the elementals, they were really on their game right now. There was almost half a cow on the picnic table, and enough sides to open up a gourmet cart at a hipster convention. His beloved mate eagerly picked up another rib to enthusiastically wave her two-filled hands under his nose. "Eating meat I am. Willingly. Joyously. Doesn't that make you happy?"

"Seeing you eat meat is always ... a good thing, mate." He punctuated his growling tone with a long kiss meant to stop her antics. Yes, he was pissed. Neither Luke nor Altea for that matter had any right to dismiss Sally's place in the council chamber. She was queen, and deserved respect. But, it was hard to maintain that mood when his female was working so hard to diffuse him.

"I would prefer you not discuss eating anything," Aquos requested.

M.J. giggled as Sally took another huge bite from the rib as she wiggled her free hand under Drake's nose. "Aww let them, I think it's cute."

Aquos got a glint in his eyes and, with a shuttered expression, handed M.J. the plate of meat, with the caramelized sauce glinting in the candlelight. "I am happy to watch you eat meat anytime as well." When the blush flooded her features, the two men burst into laughter.

"Is this what it's like? Living here? With you guys?"

Drake, Aquos and Sally shared a look of confusion. "What do you mean, my M.J.?" Aquos asked.

"This sense of camaraderie is not something I'm used to."

"We didn't have it before Sally came," Aquos said.

"I didn't do anything."

"You did everything," Drake brushed a smudge of barbecue sauce from her cheek.

"So what are you guys doing here? I mean how does it all work? Did you come in some kind of ship? Do I have to say take me to your leader? Are you here to steal our resources or have some kind of thing for anal probes?" The last one made them all break into laughter. "Oh come on, it's not that crazy to ask."

"It's not," Sally assured M.J.

"Our planet was destroyed from greed, war, and destruction. We stopped respecting our planet and turned our backs on everything we were taught by the Oracle." Drake said.

"Think: God, the Holy Ghost and Jesus combined," Sally explained.

"Doesn't sound too bad."

"In the shape of a female who happens to be Luke's mom." Sally took the final bite from the rib in her right hand and started on her left hand's rib, while her husband reverently handed her another.

"Ew … poor Luke," M.J. said. "Gives new meaning to mommy issues."

Aquos nodded at M.J.'s observation and Drake grunted. Luke's situation never had been simple and was truly far from easy. "So the world was destroyed, and the Oracle explained if we left and came here, we'd have a chance to find the keys to turn the destruction around. Resurrect our world."

Sally wiped her mouth. "They lived as separate clans on their home world for generations. When they came here, they did the same thing for thousands of years. Scattered to the wind, determined to keep distance between the clans at all costs. I can't imagine how lonely they must have been, or what you all went through. Then Luke moved them to this place, they all built Sanctuary, and he called the surviving lords to stay here and work together for the first time in their history."

Drake shook his head, "We didn't work together, love, until you came. You united us far more than Luke."

"You also brought the Mage and the Scouts back," Aquos added.

"Sounds like you have quite the fan club," M.J. said.

"The one thing I still don't get is what you think is going on with the elementals," Drake said to Aquos. "One of them actually bowed to you?"

"It was freaky." Aquos tried to explain for the two women. "They've always been obedient and happy to serve, but we were never in control of them. We've never owned them. It was always more of a synchronicity kind of thing. They needed someone to serve, and we needed people to help us."

"Did you two geniuses ever think about just asking them?"

"No," Drake and Aquos answered Sally's question simultaneously. Drake shrugged, "You know what they are like, Sally-mine. They're fine with answering questions about the house in the barest terms. They aren't one to sit down and have a chat, as you like to say. It took two hundred years before I was even sure they knew how to speak actual words, Sally-mine."

"So what do we do?"

"I guess, wait," Aquos said. "Let them come to us."

"That's what we always do," Drake nodded.

"Yeah. That doesn't work for me."

Aquos groaned. "I see a future of us trying to cook again," he shared with Drake.

"Or, the Oracle help us, actually trying to clean up after Mach and Turbo." He gestured to the beautifully set outside table, covered with multiple platters and bowls of delicious food on display. "The amount of work the elementals take on each day is monumental. A dragon couldn't manage it; a fucking squadron of dragons would fail to keep up. Don't upset the elementals, Sally-mine. We end up paying for it in so many ways I can't begin to count."

"Man up, boys," Sally quipped. She grabbed a bowl of fruit and dug into it with her fork. M.J.'s huge eyes seemed to indicate she'd never seen anyone eat like his mate before. Drake couldn't help but like the girl for the way she seemed to approve of his Sally-mine's passion for food.

"I've never known a family like you guys," M.J. muttered.

"We're a lot alike, you know. I may have had a family who raised me, but they never wanted me around. The foster care system seems a great deal like that to me from what I know about it. I didn't know what family was like until I came here. The guys here are great. I'm sorry you've seen them at their worst. Give it enough time, and you will be amazed at how wonderful it is here."

"But you belong here," M.J. sighed. "I don't."

Aquos tossed his fork to the side and stood up. He picked M.J. up without a word, and carried her away.

"Will they be alright?"

Drake cupped the back of Sally's neck and rubbed away the knot he found. "I believe Aquos is about to explain to M.J. she belongs wherever she wants to be and he is happy about that. They'll work it out, my heart."

Her eyes narrowed as she gave him a slow smile. "You want me to eat more meat, don't you?"

"I want you to eat … whatever you want." His lips caught hers before she could reach for another rib. Drake was determined to keep her mind off Aquos and his new friend, so that the two of them could find their way. This dragon's plan was to find a way to see just how much and what kinds of meat his mate felt like eating … all night long.

* * *

Mach ran into the woods, searching for the gathering place. The stand of seven ancient oak trees was a lot like a location outside of Denphan, the palace for the Speed Clan, built in the heart of Mesca.

He missed home so much it was a constant ache, just to the left of his heart's center.

Inside the trees' circle, he rang the brass bell he'd carried from the main house for just this reason. If Turbo was still out here, wandering around, trying to gather his thoughts or meditating under the stars, he would hear the bell and be forced to comply instantly.

The reaction was knit into their very souls.

Ringing the bell again, he felt the sound pick up and carry to each corner of the estate's boundaries. *Come on, Turbo. Answer, damn it.*

Nothing.

He catapulted himself to the stump remains in the circle and waited until the wind was blowing with some strength. Banging the bell as hard as his arm would manage, he hoped it would finally get picked up by Turbo's inner ear and draw him from whatever cursed hideaway he'd chosen.

When his friend, brother and only blood relative did not appear, he finally admitted defeat. Turbo wasn't responding. He knew his cousin wasn't incapacitated. He knew he was on the estate because he'd checked for his car. He knew he wasn't a hostage because Stealth had rigged them all with emergency alarms and everything was quiet on the home front.

This left one choice. Turbo wasn't responding to the call because Turbo was not Turbo anymore.

Oracle help them all if that were true.

34

"What I'd do?" M.J.'s question met with silence as Aquos continued to carry her through the darkened night. She tilted her head up against his shoulder to the stars trying to discern a difference between the diamonds strewn across dark velvet. "Can you see your planet from here? It must be so lonely to see it and not be able to return. Do you guys make wishes? There was this song once about wishing on the wrong star, it always makes me cry …" When Aquos still didn't respond, just kept plodding through the forest without speaking, she definitely started to get nervous. "Aquos … you're kind of freaking me out right now. Bad things happen to girls who wander into the forest at night, even when we're with incredibly sexy goth-boys."

"You think I'm incredibly sexy?"

"Give me a break, Aquos. You make my toes curl tighter than my hair. Let's not even start discussing what other parts of me do."

He stopped short and stared at her. The light of the moon turned his dark eyes to pool of stardust, the intense heat froze her breath. "I would definitely enjoy discussing what your other parts do, my-M.J."

"Where are you taking me, goth-boy?"

"I need you to understand something before we address your ongoing belief that you don't belong with me, M.J. I need you to see …"

"See what?"

"Everything."

His arms were hot against her back and under her knees. The silk blouse and skirt Sally had loaned her to wear was little protection against the warmth of his skin. She rested her head against his shoulder again as she mulled his words. M.J. tried not to be afraid, but it'd been so much fun. Except for the parts with the monster, things had been really great since meeting goth-boy, and she'd done things she'd never imagined she could do. Or even try. "What does *everything* mean?"

"Everything," Aquos repeated. "Everything I'm proud of, every power I possess, ever curse of my hellish existence. I want you to know it all, my love."

"How come?"

"So that if you choose to stay, you never hate me for making that choice. Because you belong with me, my M.J. I'm not sure if I'm good enough to be with you, but I don't care." He slid her down his body until she was standing in the circle of his arms. "Drake told me he showed Sally his true self before he committed his heart. You already have mine. All I'm doing right now is giving you the information you need to choose me or go back to your life."

"Goth-boy," she put her palm against his cheek and sighed. "Nothing you show me would ever make me not want you."

"Then you'll trust me," he said.

"Of course."

"Good," he turned her to the left so she could see where they'd stopped. "Then come and see my pond."

"Wait a minute, no one ever said trust had to involve water."

"You are the last person to fear water." He stepped on to the surface of the pond, and it solidified under his foot. Aquos kicked off his shoes and flipped them to the bank, as if he were standing on a wood floor. "I command this body of water, as I do all bonded hydrogen and oxygen. Come to me my heart, trust my ability, use it for your pleasure. I'll beg if I need to."

"No, goth-boy. Last thing I need you to do is beg."

The intense heat in his eyes ignited something within her. M.J. felt sexy in the glow. She grasped his hand and took her first step on the pond that looked like it stretched as far as her eyes could see. Following his lead, she toed off the flats from her feet, so she could feel the undulating water beneath the soles of her feet. She thought it would be cold like ice. It wasn't. The water was warm and welcoming, fluid against her skin, and yet held her up.

It was acceptance without changing its nature, just being there for her.

How like her goth-boy.

"My M.J. Your hair, the way it curls, reminds me of a curve in the oceans' waves. Your eyes are just as dark and sultry as water reflecting the moonlight. And your body's curves make me want to dedicate the rest of my existence to exploring their secrets. Do you have any idea how magnificent I think you are?"

"You're doing really well at telling me."

A slight tug on her hand got them moving to the center of the pond. Aquos nodded his head as if giving something permission, and the exterior suddenly shot up into the sky and joined over their heads. M.J. craned her neck back to watch it form a dome around them. "It's like standing inside a life-sized snow globe."

"Good thing or bad?"

"It's a great thing," she giggled as she turned around.

"Would you rather snow?"

M.J. shook her head. "I want whatever you want to show me, goth-boy."

The water continued to form around them until it was the sphere she was envisioning. Then Aquos did something else, and the light started to refract through the water. Color. She was now in the center of a piece of stained glass. It was the most magical thing she'd ever imagined.

"My world, my M.J. Our palace had rooms like this. Places we could live within the light. The Weather Clan had disappeared generations before I was born, so we made these meager facsimiles of what we needed. I want you, love. But I need to know you want me, you need to be willing to give me all."

"All of what?"

"Your trust. Your body. Your heart, even what you would call soul."

"It's yours," she vowed swiftly.

"Please don't think you can take it back."

"Why would I?"

He stood, just arms-length from her, trembling. The longing in his dark eyes delved into her soul and cut away the parts deadened from years of living without love. Without being wanted. She took a deep breath, and another, and smiled. "I love you, Aquos. I don't know any better words."

Then it was Aquos. Nothing but Aquos. His mouth was on hers, his breath and taste flooding her senses. His hands were hot and insistent as her clothes seemed to melt under the heat of his need. She didn't care she was standing in the middle of a pool that could be fathomless. As far as she was concerned she might as well be on solid earth. Aquos was everywhere. On top of her, inside of her. She stopped thinking of where she started and he ended. There was just them.

M.J. and goth-boy.

Lying on the bed of water, she looked up into the stars, feeling as if he'd replaced her bones with noodles. The pleasure she'd felt at his hands was mellower in the afterglow, but still as strong. "You are such a wonder."

"And you, my M.J., are a true innocent. I didn't know a female with color as dark as yours could keep blushing."

She giggled and pressed her flushed face against his chest. "I hoped it was too dark for you to see that much." When he looked down at her with one eyebrow raised, she blushed harder. "Great. My superhero can see in the dark. If you get any more awesome goth-boy I'm going to have to rethink this relationship."

"Never," he growled, tightening his arms around her.

"Never," she patted his chest.

"You would be the first to acknowledge my ..."

"Awesomeness? Powers? Prowess?" This time it was he whose face grew red with embarrassment, which sent M.J. into a new round of giggles. "Good. I want to be the first female who did so, since you were the first male who ever did anything with me at all." When he grunted with approval, she giggled again. "I do believe I just made you speechless, goth-boy."

"My M.J., you weren't just the first female. You were the first to ever say such things."

"What about your mom?"

"Died with my birth."

"And your dad?" He didn't answer her question. Aquos closed his eyes, so she shook him with concern. "What about your dad? Didn't he compliment you? Tell you how wonderful you are?"

"The blight—"

"The what?"

"Blight. It was the disease unleashed on our world when the war escalated between the clans."

"You wouldn't think water people could get sick."

"We were the first, actually. It affected my sire. Deeply. His mind grew bitter and harsh. Coming here did not help, he just got worse. My earliest memories were of him lashing out at me. As he aged, he increased in power and enmity. He started to poison everyone and anything he could get his hands on."

"That must have been awful for you."

"It was. But my father turned that hatred toward the other clans."

"What happened to him?"

"He died."

M.J. sensed from his tone there was more pain in those two words than a world full of languages could encapsulate. And yet. They were lying on a pond in the open woods, where any of the residents of sanctuary could find them, so she felt like they might as well let their souls get naked as well. "How?"

"I killed him."

"Somehow I doubt that is true."

"He was out of control." Aquos spoke fast, as if he could lessen the pain of the confession by spitting the words at her. "Luke was going to do it, but it was not his place. He was my clan. Our powers are inherited through the matriarchal line, so it was my responsibility. He'd started to take a drug he carried with him from Omega. I waited until he was unconscious, and I pulled him apart."

"What does that mean?"

Aquos moved so he was above her, his hands framing her face, his eyes delving deep in her eyes. "I waited until my father slept, and then pulled him apart on a molecular level, M.J. I then cast the essence that was him to the universe, getting the guardians of this world to spread him in the stars."

"You aren't kidding me, are you?"

"I would never lie to you about such a thing. I told you, see all of me. The good the bad, and the murderous scum who killed his only parent."

"Aquos, I assume it was bad if angel-face was going to do it."

"He was jeopardizing the compact, and had become a menace to human and Omegicon alike."

"So you didn't have a choice."

"You always have a choice, my M.J. Murder should never be an option."

M.J. bit her lip to keep the sob from escaping her at the agony she felt in his voice. Killing his father had almost killed him. She could feel it. *Fuck that, it was still killing him.* She wished she could take it away from him. She wished she could make it right. "There were kids like you in the system. Kids who had to make impossible choices for the safety of others. Even just to protect themselves. I never blamed any of them. None of us did. Why would I blame you, Aquos?"

"I thought you should know, how unworthy of you I am."

"Let me show you, goth-boy. How I feel about your worthiness." M.J. pushed him over and straddled his body. Aquos immediately slid his hands from her hips to cup her breasts, thumbing her eager nipples. She rotated her hips slightly and smiled when his shaft responded by lengthening against her. Lying over him, she stretched out her legs, rubbing her smooth skin against the crinkly hair that covered his body. "You are so … male."

"This is a good thing?"

"A great thing," she sighed. Nibbling on the stubble on his chin, she wondered why this part of his body endlessly fascinated her. Shimmying down, she moved her lips to his throat. He swallowed several times and trembled when she got to his nipples. Surprised at how much he seemed to like her suckling at them, she wondered how he'd react when she reached her destination. "If anyone here is unworthy, my goth-boy, it's me. I'm just M.J. Storm, a poor little foster girl who was lucky enough to get adopted by a kind woman before it was too late, and then unlucky enough to lose that woman to cancer. You are like some noble knight, warrior and saint all wrapped up in one toe-pointing package."

He stifled a laugh. "Toe-pointing?"

"Something they did in old timey movies. The hero would kiss the heroine and she'd bend her knee, and point her toes. That meant it was true love."

"Good to know, but I'm not worthy, my M.J., I'm just—"

She was sure he was going to say more, but his words were cut off by his loud and guttural groan. Her hands were wrapped around his cock, enjoying the feel of the warmed length that pulsed against her palms. Glancing up through her lashes at his face, she almost laughed when his eyes popped out of his head as she ran the flat of her tongue up the sensitive underside of his shaft. Good to know indeed, Omegicon anatomy worked the same way all those naughty novels said it should. She licked him all over to make sure he was as wet as she was between her legs … and dripping down her thighs.

Dipping her tongue in the hole at the top, she licked the precum over his knob as well. Then she made a tight seal with her lips, and slowly swallowed as much as she could, making Aquos curse, pray to the Oracle, and send flares of multi-colored columns of water shooting all around them. She stopped to watch the fluid fireworks he filled their world with, "Hell of a show, babe."

"M.J. if you stop again, I may just perish."

Laughing, she returned to her ministrations, thanking her stars she'd found erotic novels in her late teens and through them had found a way to vicariously learn about sex and love without having to jeopardize her own heart. Based on the amount of appreciative noises coming out of her male, she had learned truly well. When he exploded, he gave her every warning she think he could manage. He warned her many times, pulled her hair and tried to get her to stop. She didn't care.

She wanted to know what he tasted like. In the books it always sounded gross, but she wanted to know. Humans might be gross, but her goth-boy was completely and totally delicious.

When she crawled up his body, he managed to find some strength to wrap his arms around her and pull her in close. "Still think you're not worthy?"

"I do, but I'm grateful you appear to disagree with me."

He joined her laughter with his own, and something cold and small in her heart grew warm and big enough to fill a canyon. He tightened his hold around her, rubbing his palm over her back. "I'm yours, goth-boy. I still hate the monster for the way he brought us together, but right now, even he would get a pass from me for getting to know this much happiness at once."

"My M.J., as soon as some strength returns to my limbs after what you just did, I am taking you back to your room and tasting you as thoroughly as you just did me. Better rest now, because it will take all night."

"Big talk for a goth-boy, she growled.

"It's a promise from your goth-boy." Their laughter ran out through the trees, echoed back by the roar of a wild animal far in the distance.

 35

M.J. gave the air a fist bump and shimmied her hips when she saw what was on the other side of the swinging door. Finally. She'd found the kitchen. It had only taken twenty minutes of wandering the mansion and opening every door she'd come across. She chuckled when she considered how lucky she was that she hadn't uncovered something she didn't want to see. Like someone going to the bathroom or having sex. Though, come to think of it, didn't the guys say there was only one female here, when she was in the car? That was Sally. So she should be safe.

Just in case, she would ask Aquos about it later.

Inside the kitchen, she returned to her random open door strategy, the same she'd employed throughout her childhood in one foster home after another, determined to find the pantry. There had to be some kind of cabinet filled with food in a house this freaking large. Right?

She needed something spicy and preferably greasy. Keeping a goth-boy happy really gave a girl an appetite.

Most of the interiors had pots, pans, dishes, glasses and utensils. The first large door she tried had a bathroom. The next had shelves with silver and big serving dishes. The last had … a girl? "Hello. I'm M.J."

The girl, in her mid-twenties, had long dark hair, and was dressed in black jeans, a hoodie and some kind of odd leather shoes that were laced to right under her knees. M.J. noticed her hands filled with boxes of cereal, the large sack at her feet partially filled. She suddenly understood what she had just walked into. Years of being in the foster care system had taught her more than she realized. "If you need food, it's okay. I won't tell. I'd love to know your name, though."

"Avaris. I am called Avaris."

"Nice to meet you, Avaris. If you have any problems with the guys here, just ask for me or Aquos. We'll cover for you. I promise."

"Why?"

"Why what?"

"Why would you help me?"

"I know what it's like to be hungry, Avaris. I understand desperation even more. You need help, just let me know."

"Th—" Avaris swallowed hard as if saying the word got stuck in her throat.

"You're welcome," M.J. winked at her. "Now, how about you pass me those wasabi flavored potato chips and I'll let you finish."

Avaris handed over the bag and M.J. closed the door. She understood pride only too well. If the girl needed help, she'd have to ask for it. From what M.J. could see, whoever Avaris was and for whatever reason she was stealing food in the middle of the night, it seemed like she had things well in hand.

Besides, there had been way too many times she'd had to do the same. At least this place was well able to handle the theft.

Trying to re-trace her steps back to her man and their insanely comfortable bed, M.J. took a wrong turn and ended up in a huge room with soaring ceilings. Just one of the six chandeliers would have filled her bedroom; she had never imagined someone could build a space so large. It had to be a ballroom, but who needed a ballroom nowadays? She wondered how they even heated it, when she noticed it was filled.

With people. Dressed in the long robes the elementals favored, M.J.'s mouth fell open with surprise at how many had gathered in one space. "Hello."

They all faced her as if they had a hive mind, fell to their knees, and pressed their foreheads to the floor. *Crap. Not this again.* "I'm M.J.," she said. "I think I've seen one or two of you around, though it was only briefly. Wait, one was called Tana. She seemed really nice, I told Aquos and Sally how impressive you all are."

No response.

"I know I'm not from your planet, but I am really happy to meet you."

The deafening quiet in the room felt harsh to her, and she suddenly really wished she had some kind of Miss Manners equivalent for the Omegicon. Maybe she was violating some kind of religious ceremony or private time? What if she was being disrespectful right now? This was the last thing she wanted. Sanctuary may be in the middle of Pennsylvania, but she imagined this place was sort of like an embassy, which meant she was basically on Omega soil.

116

Omega probably had all kinds of protocol rules you were supposed to follow, depending on the clans.

Rules that she probably had just broken.

She backed out of the room, the crinkling sounds from the foil bag she clutched sounding like thunder in the oppressive silence.

"M.J."

"Aquos," she rushed into his arms and released her held breath. "Come with me. You've got to make them stop," she grabbed his hand and dragged him back into the ballroom. "No one should have to do this."

They entered the room, which was empty. Where the hell did they go?

"My M.J. … are you well?"

"They were right here." She rushed over to one of the floor length windows and looked outside into the dark night. "They were all right here."

"Love … what is it? How may I assist?"

"Your servant people. They were all in here."

He dragged her away from the window and wrapped his arms around her. "Now you're worrying me. What's wrong?"

She sighed and closed her eyes. "Maybe I was hallucinating?"

"Why would you be hallucinating?"

"I don't know. But nothing explains … wait, do the elementals have powers like you? Can they all just disappear with a blink of their eyes or something?"

"The elementals' only power seems to be a love of constantly working, sweet. I can honestly state in thousands of years I have never witnessed one of them blinking their eyes, or any other ability. Why? What did you see?"

"Nothing," she tried to smile to make him not worry, but could still see concern in his eyes. "I'm fine."

"You are many things—" Whatever he was going to say was interrupted by the chirping of the cell phone still in his back pocket. "That's weird," he reached for the phone. "Only one who ever calls me on this blasted thing is Mach, and I know he's inside the house right now. I don't know this number." He showed the display to M.J. "Do you?"

"Squirt," she grabbed it from him and answered in the same breath.

"M.J.," the voice on the other side was so loud Aquos could hear it clearly. "They're coming for me. I don't know what to do."

"Hide," M.J. yelled into the phone. "We're coming. Hold on, Squirt. We're coming." She hung up and looked at him in regret as he took the phone from her. "Aquos I have to go. Is there a car service or someone I can call?"

Aquos was already texting before she finished the question. He braided their fingers together as he started moving briskly through the hall. "Don't be ridiculous, love. Where you go, so do I. I've already asked the guys to help. Whatever army or problem you face, we do so together."

She closed her eyes in thanks as she let him lead, silently sending a prayer that whatever Squirt was facing would wait until they got there.

36

When they got to the entrance of the mansion, Mach, Blade and Stealth were all waiting for them next to the car. "I can't ask you all to go," Aquos said.

"You aren't asking," Blade opened the passenger side door.

Stealth wrenched at the shotgun door with a triumphant expression. Clearly, he'd won the coin toss. "We're volunteering. Now, who or what are we killing, and who's telling Luke so he doesn't ground our asses?"

"M.J., tell Mach where we're going." Aquos got into the back with M.J. sandwiched between him and Blade. He hid his pleasure when she slid closer to him, not wanting her body to touch the warrior's. On Omega, no female would do such a thing, they'd be honored the noble stoic warrior class chose them, if only to touch. He couldn't help feeling flattered by her clear preference. Trying to hide his emotions, he put his arm around her as she gave Mach directions.

When they arrived at the broken down racetrack, his pleasures did a complete one eighty. Before he was brimming with pride and pleasure, now he was fighting a sense of despair. This is where his woman lived? His eyes took in the peeling paint, the open pits of refuse and barrels of toxic chemicals.

His M.J. can't live here. It wasn't good enough to be her garbage dump, much less her actual home.

But they'd just met and he knew from Sally that humans didn't move as fast as his clan did. From the stories his father left with him, he and his mother had married the same day they met. They knew their match as soon as they'd looked into each other's eyes. It was that simple.

Nothing was simple here.

Aquos was sure that he belonged with M.J. He wasn't as sure she'd agree.

"Squirt," M.J. screamed as she jumped out of the car and went running into a garage. "Squirt."

"You sure she isn't Speed Clan?" Mach asked, looking at the partially cannibalized cars in the garage bay. M.J. continued to scream for her foster sibling as she went tearing up a ramshackle set of wood stairs. "She obviously likes fast."

"M.J. is mine."

His statement was met with grunts of approval and curt nods from Stealth and Blade. Mach just gestured to the garage with a raised eyebrow. When Aquos started to growl, he quickly held up his palm. "Cool, bro. We're good. I'm indebted to her anyway. But Luke wanted to know whose clan she belonged to, and it seems …"

"Mine."

"Yes, caveman. I got it, the girl is yours."

"I, for one, am digging this new authoritative Aquos," Blade said.

Stealth smiled, actually smiled at him. "Looks good, A."

M.J. came downstairs and flew into Aquos's arms. "I can't find her."

"I thought your Squirt was a male."

"No," she looked up at him confused, "why would you think that?"

Aquos nodded at Stealth. "Can you help?"

"If it is just a female we are looking for, there appears to be someone hiding in the tool cabinet in the far corner of this room."

Aquos nodded with appreciation at Stealth. The Air Clan's abilities to see through walls was always something that came in handy. He also was the one who was the closest to the elementals and the Mage Clan. So without them they would have had no ability to stabilize the tesseract and would be utterly lost in their own filth.

They'd still be living better than his female.

M.J. squeaked, ran to the cabinet and wrenched it open. Inside, Aquos could see a girl in her late teens, with a dirty khaki hat on, black t-shirt, and jeans so faded they should have been white though the oil stains made it more like a Dalmatian hide. The figure catapulted out of the enclosed space, wrapping itself around M.J. as if it were a coat. "M.J." the girl whimpered into her neck.

"It's okay, Squirt. I brought reinforcements."

"Why did I think we were searching for a little boy?"

"So did I," Blade shared with Stealth.

"Really not hating it being a hot female," Mach said.

Aquos moved closer to M.J. trying to decide if he should feel jealous or happy for their reunion. He felt unease in his heart, though. This did not feel like it boded well for his plans for having M.J. move in with him. Luke had been quite clear about the Earth guardian's sentiments on the Omega interfering with the Earthers. They were not allowed to interfere and were supposed to limit interaction. The guys had all taken to finding females to hook up with outside of Sanctuary's walls, and that was fine. Bringing one, and it looked like where M.J. went so too did Squirt, so bringing two to live in the mansion would probably be big on the no-no list with the archangels.

Shit. Well, being happy had been fun for a hot fucking minute.

"Squirt, come meet Aquos."

"You finally got yourself a guy?" The creature M.J. clearly loved more than herself, based on her not even acknowledging the dirt and oil that was transferred onto her person from their embrace, came bouncing over to him. "Are you a good guy or do I need to kick you in the nuts?"

"Wow. How to answer that question, huh A?"

"It's a pleasure to meet you," Aquos ignored Mach's question and held out his hand to the girl standing before him. She kept shifting from foot-to-foot, her eyes squinting up at him. He guessed she was a little over five feet, a veritable midget by their standards, but there was something about her eyes and attitude that made her seem like she was ten feet tall. "I swear I treat M.J. as a delicate treasure."

Squirt snorted with laughter, then sobered up and gave him a horrified look. "She'd hate that. M.J. really needs someone who lets her be her."

"I cherish your sister, just the way she is."

"Then your nuts are safe."

Mach laughed so hard, tears streamed from his eyes. "That's got to be a relief."

"Squirt," M.J. turned her around to face her again. "What happened? Why were you hiding? What's going on? It isn't Razor is it? I thought I'd have at least a couple of days before the race prep began."

"There were some scary guys here." Squirt looked down at her feet as she swallowed hard. "I just … I got scared."

"What about these humans frightened you?"

Squirt tilted her head all the way back so she could look into Blade's eyes. "You are really tall. And ripped. Are you a weight lifter or something? I always wanted to study a power lifter to see what effect their blood distribution had on the tension in the muscles to see if that could improve the tires—"

"Focus, Squirt!"

The girl looked at M.J. blinked a few times, and then blushed. Aquos realized that her pale skin and violet colored eyes was probably quite prized in this world. It seemed a pale facsimile of beauty when compared with the vivid tones of his M.J.

"Apologies," she offered to the room. Looking at Blade, she blushed, "I like cars, and any way I can make them go faster or be more efficient ..."

"You've done naught wrong, Lady Squirt."

"Lady Squirt?" She elbowed M.J. and did that little dance on her toes again. Aquos realized it was easy to see this was one female who despised standing still. "I like that. The humans scared me because they were big, though not as big as you, and carrying really scary looking guns. Now, any gun is scary when you don't have one, I think maybe they are even when you do have one, as long as you have a bigger gun is maybe the only time it isn't scary, but you can never be sure—"

"Squirt," M.J. yelled at the same time she put her hand over the girl's mouth to slow her verbal torrent, "you're scaring the boys."

When M.J. slowly withdrew her fingers from her face, the girl's cheeks were blazing with color. "I do that," she confessed to the room. "M.J. says I can't help it, because when I'm really into inventing something I don't talk for days so I always feel I have to make up for lost time."

The squeal of tires outside could be heard inside the building. Doors slammed, then Luke, Tamar and Drake came running into the garage.

"Oooh, more really big guys. Think one of them would let me measure their blood response?" When M.J. just shook her head and covered her face, Squirt pouted. "I don't know why not; it's not like it's an invasive test."

"What is amiss?"

"Lady M.J., you are dragon and should not be without proper escort," Tamar intoned.

Drake rolled his eyes, "I assume that means you and no one else."

"I would think you would be busy guarding your Queen from the pursuit of Ser Hunter," Tamar said.

"My Queen has no interest in Hunter."

"Then I shall find a different suitor for her."

"Where have you been, exactly?" Squirt eyed Tamar's armor with calculated interest. "Or should I say when?"

M.J. just shook her head. "It's really sweet of all of you to come ..."

Aquos went to put his arm around her, glanced at Squirt and chose instead to tuck his hands into his jean pockets. "M.J.'s Squirt appears to have been menaced by several large human strangers."

"We shall make sure they are gone," Drake stated, glancing at Tamar.

Luke said, "We'll search the exterior structures for any men. You and M.J. should make sure this building is safe."

Mach winked at Squirt, who straightened up as most young females would at the handsome speedster's attention. "Lady Squirt, perhaps you would like to accompany me? You can tell me if we find your interloper and I'll impress you with how swiftly we can dissuade them from troubling you again."

"And I will go to chaperone you two," Stealth offered.

Blade shook his head. "Guess I'll go to make sure Mach can actually dissuade whatever or whoever they find. Otherwise we shall be stuck having to save him next." The others chuckled as they separated to handle their assignments.

37

M.J. stood awkwardly while Aquos meticulously opened every door and cabinet in the garage. She couldn't help comparing what the track looked like, with it's peeling paint and stained concrete. A sad step down from the mansion stuffed with antiques and oiled wood paneling. If she remembered some of the rooms she'd wandered through when searching for the kitchen, there were not one but multiple chambers lined with silk.

Not to mention the fricking ballroom.

Crap. She was poor.

"Are there any other doors to the upstairs?"

"This is the only way in or out," she answered.

He took her hand and led the way up the ramshackle stairs. Untreated wood, nails partially sticking out, even long peels of paint on the wall. She'd never go without shoes in her own home. She also bought a small fortune in anti-bacterial gels each week from the discount store.

The apartment had been redone with the few pieces they were able to rescue from Squirt's mom's house before the eviction. Her big rose colored sofa was on the far wall, the rocking chair next to it with the faded blue and green flowers Squirt's mom had painted on it when she was pregnant with Squirt. They couldn't find a coffee table, so covered some old wood crates with a sage green sheet. The television sat on cases of motor oil. M.J. painted vivid landscapes on the walls to make up for the abysmal view of the track outside the windows. More old sheets hung by nails in place of curtains. The table and chairs were some kind of horrid laminate older than the track.

Stepping into the kitchen, she sighed. When Aquos gave her an interested look, she explained. "Squirt must not be eating. It's too clean in here."

"You do everything for her, don't you?"

"Of course." His eyes slid away from her as if they were greased and she knew something bad must be going through his mind. She just didn't know what it was. Aquos took her hand again and led her through the rest of the pitifully tiny apartment. Squirt's bedroom, the walls covered with blueprints and doodles for future inventions, the bed unmade and the floor piled with clothing that would never see the inside of a dresser or closet. Bathroom with the same fixtures from the 1920s, the year the track was built and the last time anyone beside M.J. had cared about it. Finally, they entered her room.

She bit her lip as she tried to decide what he was seeing, or even, feeling.

Her queen-sized bed was made, the hand-sewn quilt a gift from Squirt's mom when she'd first come to live with her. The bedside tables were filled with sketch pad and art books, the lamp on top a 1940s art deco treasure she had found on the street. Everything else was put away.

"M.J.," Aquos touched one of the walls with a reverent sigh. "This is…"

"What? Horrible? Terrible? What?"

Turning to her, his eyes were wide with shock. "You don't know?"

"Know what?"

Aquos ran his hand over the wall. M.J. tried to figure out what had struck him speechless. She'd painted an ocean at night, with a beach covered with pure white sand. The sky was almost purple, the stars and planets glowing against it. In the distance, you could see blueberry mountains, with cherry red sailboats gliding into the horizon. "It's my home," he explained. "This is Omega, the way I was told it was, centuries before the blight."

"Goth-boy, that's not possible."

"Hells it isn't. Those mountains are Peleos, M.J., the birthplace of the elementals and gem warriors. We have legends of the great Weather Clan lords, the originators of everything on our world. And this is my home ocean, Tindaridai. You even included the Sandkerk; these ships are what the Air Clan used to travel between the clans to their homes in the hidden lands."

"It's just something I saw in my dreams."

Aquos snatched her up and kissed her. She melted in his embrace, his heat, his taste, the feeling of him, how much he wanted her. It felt like the start of everything all over again.

Yet, she had the painful feeling, it also meant good-bye.

"M.J., we cannot doubt the guardian anymore. You are Omega."

"But how? I don't understand. We have genetic testing here; would that help?"

"You get your genes tested and we'll all end up in some government lab. I guess we just have to wait and see what happens, but there's one thing..."

"I'm not going to like this, am I?"

Aquos shook his head. "We cannot be together until we know."

"How come?"

"There are rules for the Omega. Until we know what clan you belong to, you cannot foreswear yourself to another."

"Seriously, goth-boy? What fucking century do you think this is?"

"M.J., I'd rather save us some hurt right now than a world of hurt later."

It took a few minutes for her to breathe air again. *How could he not know?* Losing him even a little right now already felt like a world of pain. "You told me that night on the pond, there would be no take backs. You told me you were showing me all of you and I had to swear not to withdraw my heart and soul. How could you do this? How could you pull me apart like this?"

"You don't know our ways. This is for the best."

"Bull shit. It's certainly not for my best, Aquos. Don't do this."

"You can have anything—"

"I want you. How can you not want me, too?"

"M.J., this is for the best. Mistakes like this cost us our world. I won't be party to such a thing again. You have to decide who you want."

"I want you. I won't say it again."

"Then you need to decide who you belong to. Until you know where you're from how can you possible know where you should be going? Tell me I'm wrong. Tell me you aren't longing for a family."

"You were supposed to be my family, remember?"

"Can you honestly say you don't wish you had more?"

Luke came running into the room before M.J. could respond. Which was probably a good thing, since her first thought was to kill her goth-boy, or, at least beat him to within an inch of his life. "M.J.," angel-face gasped, "come quick."

Glad he hadn't bothered to notice her otherworld painting, Luke dragged her with Aquos trailing, out of the garage and straight to her studio. *Super. They might as well have gone through her underwear drawer.* It would have felt a lot less like an invasion of privacy. She glanced at Squirt who just shrugged helplessly as he dragged her inside. When they were in the shed, she was surprised to see the rest of the Omega, except for the two dragons, with their arms immersed in the dust bags she'd left in the middle of the work space. "What is this?"

"When I polish my sculptures it makes dust. You guys are playing with the trash bags of that debris. Which is a little weird ..."

"Is this what you had all over your hair and dress when Turbo found you?"

"Kidnapped, Luke." Aquos glowered at him. "He kidnapped her."

Luke shrugged off Aquos's censure and picked up a handful of the fine grains of sand. "Is it? I'm sorry if this seems odd to you, M.J. We've never encountered this before, and for some reason, it reminds us of home."

Aquos looked around with his eyes widening, "This is what you do? This is your art?"

She tried again to imagine what he was seeing. Tried to see it through his eyes. The small wood building was lined with shelves. A single bulb lit the space. She had the polisher set in the corner with a low wooden stool beside it. Other than that, there was nothing but the pieces she labored over. "It is." She picked up one of the glass pieces and let the light refract in it's clear depths. "I go to a small beach in Delaware every other month or so when I hear there will be a good storm. The lightning hits the wet sand and makes fulgurite. I polish it until it looks like this."

"Did any of you know about this?" Luke asked.

The guy all shook their heads at Luke's question. Aquos picked up one of the pieces that resembled a dancing cloud in his eyes. "Your art takes lightning and makes it into something you can hold." He turned to her and smiled, making her toes clench as a wave of longing almost swamped her. "How like you."

"Can we have this?"

"Of course," M.J. answered Luke. "I'm happy to give you guys the statues too, if it will help."

"No," Aquos's quick reply stopped everyone else from what they were going to say. "The bags of your refuse is more than enough of a help. If you guys dump it in the pool or one of the hot tubs it might be best. It's what seemed to help me. I would, however, really like to keep this one."

"You can have anything you want." Her eyes flared as she stared at him, hoping he got that by anything, she really meant anyone.

"My deepest thanks," he bowed slightly.

The other guys each hefted a bag over their shoulders. "I can't believe how much better I feel," Blade muttered. Staring at M.J., he also gave a brief bow, "The Warrior Clan is eternally in your debt."

All she could do was stare at Aquos, who refused to look her in the face. "Don't worry about it. I'll make more tomorrow."

"We must go, Aquos stated.

"You don't. You really don't."

"If you ever need me," he glanced at her, his eyes fell to the ground and he left. M.J. almost cried out in protest that he didn't even kiss her good-bye.

"M.J., if I did something …"

"You didn't," she told Luke. "Take care of him for me, would you?"

He nodded and also left. Squirt came in and wrapped her arms around her before she hit the ground, as the grief hit her with a tangible force. Her head fell forward, the pain so great she couldn't even cry. He left. He said doing it this way would save them both from a world of pain later.

Little did he know, she was feeling a galaxy of it now.

38

One thing she could not escape was Razor and his never-ending list of shit that needed to be done. The next day she and Squirt were hard at work cleaning the driver bunkhouse, a chore Squirt had managed to put off during what she liked to call M.J.'s fuck-ation.

Her mom would wash both of their mouths out with soap.

She didn't know what was worse. The pain she felt at Aquos leaving, or the worried little glances Squirt kept sending her way.

They were sitting outside the garage enjoying peanut butter and jelly sandwiches, when the car drove up. "I think that's for you," Squirt drawled at the shiny Range Rover filled with the two dragon knights. She started to try and brush some of the dirt from her face and hands, but quickly realized some things were a lost cause.

"Greetings, Lady M.J.," Ser Hunter gave a flourishing bow.

"Oh, I'm loving this," Squirt said.

"Greetings to the young Squirt," Tamar added.

"How come I'm young Squirt and she's Lady M.J.?"

"Apologies, miss, but Lady M.J. is a dragonswan as declared by our queen so she must be addressed by her proper title."

"M.J. is a what now? A dragon?" Squirt smacked M.J.'s side. "Where the hell have you been?"

"Pennsylvania," she snapped. "Why are you guys here?"

Hunter returned to the car and pulled out a large cooler, and then piled a huge box on top of it. Tamar gestured to the bounty, "We come bearing gifts from our Queen Salvation as well as your elementals."

"They're not mine."

"I suggest you tell them that," Hunter said. "Where shall I put this?"

"Anywhere you want," Squirt was busy eyeing the dragon knight's muscles, which made M.J. elbow her. "What?"

"Stop trying to figure out how you can use him for your experiment."

"How come?"

"It's rude, Squirt. You know that."

"Actually, my lady, we would be honored to stay here for a few hours if it suits you both."

"How come?"

The two dragons both appeared sheepish all of a sudden. "It would seem to be the best course of action."

M.J. suddenly guessed what happened, "How bad did you piss off the Queen?"

"Our Queen appears to take umbrage at our teasing her consort."

"Because the two of you refuse to acknowledge her consort is her husband?"

"True, Lady M.J., but in my opinion, he takes things far too seriously."

M.J. laughed at Tamar's umbrage. "Fine. You guys are welcome to stay until things die down at Sanctuary."

"Where have you been?"

"You did not tell young Squirt of your adventure?"

"There hasn't been time."

Hunter hefted the boxes up farther to adjust his hold. "You were here all last night. Alone. Something no dragonswan should be."

"I wasn't alone, I had Squirt."

"Who listened to her cry all night, so if you guys can help explain what happened, and who I have to kill, I would appreciate it."

Realizing she'd left poor Ser Hunter carrying two large boxes, that now would be the perfect time to break everyone up, M.J. decided to take some control. "Ser Hunter and Tamar, please come with me. Squirt, you can go and finish the straightening up in the bunk house so that Razor doesn't get pissed."

"Fine," Squirt started to back-up with an impish look in her eyes. "But I'll get the story from them sooner or later."

"Does she go far?"

"She'll be fine; follow me gentlemen." M.J. didn't want the two knights anywhere near her little foster sister, or for that matter, for Squirt to be near the knights. Stuck finishing the bunkhouse was a fitting punishment for all the work she'd stuck on M.J. in the last few months. Leading them into the apartment, she pointed to the table. "Do you know what's in the boxes?"

"Queen Salvation sent clothing for you and Squirt," Hunter explained.

"Her consort refuses to let her leave Sanctuary so she gets even through judicious use of something called retail revenge."

"Perfectly understandable." M.J.'s giggles turned to oohs when she saw what was in the box. Clothes. Beautiful clothes. As she pulled out the fine silk and linen, she looked in shock to the two dragons. "This is too much."

"Queen Salvation was quite adamant, and informed us it would be a travesty of untold reckoning if we dared to return with any of it."

M.J. shook her head at Tamar's grave tone. "You guys are hilarious."

"We're dragons," Hunter said. When Tamar and M.J. both gave him a smile, he shrugged. "Well, we are."

"Please tell Sal—I mean Queen Salvation, we thank her."

"Our pleasure," they spoke in unison and bowed.

Moving the now empty box, Sally opened the cooler. Food. Bins upon bins of food. She opened up one of the containers and enjoyed breathing in the delicious aroma of basil pesto marinated vegetable salad. "I don't understand, the elementals think we starve out here?"

"I believe they are concerned about your well-being," Tamar said.

Hunter snorted. "The two that handed the cooler to me said peanuts and sugared fruit don't make a lunch."

"What?"

"They said peanuts and sugar—"

"No, I mean how did they know what we would have for lunch?"

Both the knights shrugged at her query. "The elementals are the oldest of our kind. None of us are sure where their originator clan has gone to, they disappeared generations before the blight. So none of us are clear on any of their abilities or powers. Perhaps they feel bonded to you."

"Aquos mentioned that clan bonds are important."

"They are everything," both dragons answered.

"Right. I should probably show you something," she confessed to Tamar.

He gave her a gentle smile, "Sally and I were hoping you would volunteer."

"Is that food?" Squirt came bouncing in and made her way directly to the cooler. She was eating from the pasta salad container with her hands before anyone could say anything.

"Damnit, Squirt, show some manners." The girl looked up at them with a face covered with what appeared to be a creamy dill dressing. M.J. grabbed the napkins and the old coffee can they used to store their cutlery. "Gentlemen, would either of you like something to eat? I'm sure Squirt would be happy to share." The look the girl gave her was so clearly one of outrage, everyone laughed in response. "Well, maybe happy was a little extreme."

"Perhaps I can keep young Squirt company while you share your bedroom with Ser Tamar?"

"You're gonna sleep with him, too?"

M.J. closed her eyes and tried counting to a hundred before she attempted to face the two dragon knights. Neither of them were laughing, but she sensed the amusement they had to feel. One thing she could say about Squirt. Nothing could stop her or change her from being ... well, Squirt. Which always made her love her just a little more. "No Squirt. Ser Tamar just wants to see the painting in my room. Try not to scare Hunter off, ok?"

"I won't," Squirt promised.

"And do not ask him to volunteer for your experiment," M.J. said noting the shrewd look in her sister's eyes.

"Fine." Squirt's answer was enough to get her to pause when she heard her sister mutter something about her being a spoilsport. Tamar put his hand on her back to get her started again.

Inside her room, M.J. waited to see what Tamar would say.

Silence.

"You're killing me here, dude," she said.

"Apologies, Lady M.J., but were I actually killing you, I believe you would be screaming, not drawling your words."

"What do you think?"

"I think you are an extraordinary artist. This is just as I remember it." He looked at her with eyes wide and full of wonder. "What are you?"

"You have no idea how much I wish I knew."

"We had best find out," Tamar touched the painting again and shook his head. "We had best find out fast."

39

Hours later, Luke was sitting with Sally when the two knights returned from their mission. They had a movie on, but had been discussing the odd behavior of the elementals. Other than preparing the cooler for M.J., the clans that kept everything working in Sanctuary had been curiously disappearing. Luke had no idea what to do about it, and Sally was exhausted from directing the Clan Lords on cooking all day. When she saw her weary and disheveled knights coming in the front door she almost jumped off the couch. "Is she okay?"

"Your dragonswan seems well," Hunter bowed and turned on his heel quickly to leave.

"What's wrong with him?"

"Drake threatened to kill him if he found Hunter near me again," Sally explained.

"Actually, your consort threatened to pull his entrails out of his nose," Tamar corrected.

"Shouldn't you be calling me your majesty and bowing?"

"Can't," Tamar collapsed on the couch. "Your adopted dragon exhausted me. Those females do more work in a day than the entire squadron completes in a week. I didn't know I could be so tired." His nose crinkled and he gave a small shudder. "Or dirty, for that matter."

"Did you discover anything of relevance?"

"The Water Lord is correct. The painting is of Omega. Whatever or whoever the female is, she belongs on Sanctuary grounds."

"Is she dragon? Like for real?"

"My apologies, your majesty, if Lady M.J. was dragon born, I would sense her kaji. Now, I willingly do whatever penance you deem worthy, but I leave to infiltrate your Drake's hidden spring so I may take a proper bath."

"Go ahead, but when Drake has a cow, I'm sending him to you."

"Watching your consort have a cow would give me no end of pleasure," Tamar stated on his way out of the room.

"Super." Sally threw her hands up. "If this kid comes out of the egg with his fingers in his ears I won't be surprised. The three of them seem to be determined to drive me out of my mind."

"Of course they are," Luke chuckled. "Their squabbles serve to keep you distracted."

She released a heavy sigh. "What are you going to do?"

"I don't know. M.J.'s fulgurite dust has been helping stabilize all the Clan Lords now—"

"All of them but you."

"How did you know?"

Sally brushed her fingertips against the corner of his right eye and over his forehead. "You show lines at the corners here, and there's a vein in on the side here that is beating so fast I could dance a cha cha cha to it."

"I have no idea what this cha thing is."

"Not good," Sally said. "So what are you going to do?"

"There's nothing I can do."

"What about the Oracle?"

"She's not taking calls right now."

"What do you mean ... she's not taking calls?"

He just shook his head. "Sally, if something happens to me, I need you to know you are the only one who can take over. The Oracle will accept you, she's always had a soft spot for the dragons, it's why she gave them control of the tesseract. But the Clan Lords will need someone to handle their fights and keep them focused on finding the rest of the answers to the prophecy. It's got to be you."

"Luke," she leaned forward and took his hands in hers. "Nothing is going to happen to you."

He thought about the horrible burning he felt when he'd tried to insert his hand into the tesseract light. The one thing that should never happen to the Light Clan was to be rejected by the portal. It was made of their energy. He couldn't tell her that, though. He was much too ashamed. "Just promise me. Please."

"Of course, but don't you think Stealth—"

"Too many inner conflicts with the others."

"Blade?"

"The Warrior Clan believe in battling through all obstacles first and last."

"I won't even bother suggesting the speedsters; how about Drake?"

"He's about to go into nesting mode to protect your young. Besides, Drake's only priority is your happiness and the safety of your king. He won't be able to put aside his personal imperatives for the good of our people."

"Luke …"

"Your vow, Queen Salvation. I gave you Sanctuary once, well, that vow goes two ways. I now require your vow that you will take the crystal throne should I fall."

She closed her eyes and swallowed hard.

"My love?"

"I'm fine, Drake." Sally held up her hand and Drake moved from the entrance to take it, wrapping himself around her body to leave one hand in hers and the other over her stomach where their child grew. "Luke, if you truly need my vow for your peace of mind, you have it. But I swear we will do anything we need to in order to safeguard your future."

Luke took her free hand and held it to his forehead. "You are a magnificent Queen; I just want you to know that." When he released her, Sally shared a look with him that she turned to her fingers. *She felt it. Good.* The transfer was done, the bond was made.

"I tell her every day, angel-face."

He groaned, and patted Sally's knee. The Omega would be safe under the rule of this kind-hearted woman. "I see that nickname isn't going away anytime soon."

"Nope. You're stuck with it."

He smiled at Drake and Sally, and rose slowly to make sure he appeared steady on his feet, starting to leave. "That was what I feared."

"Luke, we would help if you would but ask."

He flinched, glad that the couple could not see the pain their words caused him. To be so weak. In need of assistance and earn others' pity; it left him with a worse case of nausea than the pain in his head. "There is no help. And I fear I have long since grown too old for hope."

Luke kept going, not willing even to turn around to see how his words were met by the couple. He was happy they had found each other. No other being had as much honor as the dragon, and Drake had faced centuries of ostracism from his kind. His joining with Salvation had given the man a new peace, and the rest of them got to enjoy it, if at least vicariously.

Outside, he kept moving until he made it to the ancient oak trees they had found as a way to mark this place as where they should build Sanctuary. Back then, this place was still under the rule of England and a young man named George was just learning how to use his father's axe, or so legend said.

Collapsing by the stump where Sally and Drake were married, he craned his head back so he could stare at the cloudy night sky above him.

The silence and darkness became as a cloak, one he wished he could wrap around him as comforting as the embrace of a lover. "I'm ready," he confessed to the void. "I'm ready to die. I'm tired of this fight. I am so weary of the pain. Let me go. I did what I could for the Omega. Sally will lead them far better than I ever could. Please," he wondered if he was praying to the Earthers' God or to the Omega Oracle or even to his mother. And then he wondered, just what made the difference between those three titles. He closed his eyes and prepared for the release, the shedding of his physical form for something ethereal. "It's time for me to die."

"Why would you say such a thing?"

Luke expected the female voice to belong to Gabrielle. Instead, , when he opened his eyes he found his longtime friend ... he jumped to his feet with surprise, and fell on his ass when his body collapsed.

"Hello."

"Are you real?"

"Of course I am," she answered. Her long dark hair, black sweater and jeans were visible in the cold clarity of the night's glow. Luke felt his heart cartwheel when he looked upon the fragile features of her face and her silky ebony hair. "Why do you want to die?"

"I've been ill," he explained.

She nodded and glanced over her shoulders uneasily. "I could sense it."

"Why did you run away? When I gave you sanctuary, I meant it. You didn't have to run."

"There were others who waited for me. I had already stayed too long that night."

"I thought you left because the mercenaries attacked us." He began to cough, a deep racking sound that felt as if it rattled his bones. "I was so worried I would never find you again."

"They who care the most call me the Avaris. You may do the same if you wish." She tilted her head and seemed to fly across the clearing to sit beside him. He longed to reach out and touch her knee, but was terrified she would disappear into the mist like last time. "I was always here. You granted me sanctuary so I stayed close, but there are others I must answer to."

He was going to tell her how much he understood, but another round of racking coughs hit him, along with the escalation of the pounding in his head, which made him a quivering, groaning mess.

"Drink this." A vial was pressed to his lips and he eagerly swallowed it down. It was as if a switch flipped in his body. The fluid immediately turned it off, and Luke felt like himself once more. He could feel the power from the starlight bathing him, bent the beams from the moon to reach them, and he could see his Avaris in full for the first time. She was as beautiful as he remembered, more so actually. Dressed in dark clothes, her cloth boots were a style he hadn't seen since his youth. Her hair was a silken curtain he wished he could feel against his face. "Better?"

Before he could respond, a crack of thunder sounded and the girl whirled around in a defensive posture to protect him. "What was that?"

The light disappeared; the moon and stars were still in the sky but they no longer illuminated the clearing. Luke reached out to grasp her arm, but she shook him off. Then, half a dozen, ten-foot towering creatures appeared, surrounding them as if they were points on a clock's face. Each was a different jewel color swirled with gold, their faces twisted with hateful malice. Barely faces, he could hardly discern eyes from mouths and noses. They carried swords that glowed with an unearthly light, and pointed the razor sharp weapons directly at them.

"He is friend," Avaris said.

The creatures each took a step forward. Luke tried to move to protect the girl instead, but the weapons were so close he recognized any movement would endanger them both. "Let me help."

"You can't," she pushed Luke back down, forcing him to appear to cower. "This is the one who gave me sanctuary. He is friend to the one known as M.J. You cannot do it. Your intention is against our code, so I demand you stand down."

They did not waver, and Luke gulped, recognizing the death he had just asked for might now actually arrive.

Unfortunately, he no longer had any interest in it.

"I'll stay with you. Nothing has changed." Avaris slowly rose and the swords were withdrawn a hairs-breadth for fear of hurting her. "His life has been paid for by the M.J. We know him through her action. You know the code."

The swords were withdrawn. The creatures stepped back.

Avaris turned to him and gave him a regretful shrug. "No more death for you, my Luke. Tell M.J. we gave our thanks the only way we knew how."

With those simple words, she disappeared into the night.

And once more, Luke could see the stars and moonlight. He bounded to his feet, recognizing it was past time to get some answers.

40

M.J. stood up and leaned back, trying to stretch her muscles from being hunched over for so long. Razor demanded there be hand-rolled pretzels for the kids who came to the track and that meant loads of prep. They made the dough the night before, today they were supposed to roll them and leave the trays with the prepped dough for the catering crew to cook during the race.

Speaking of they, where the hell was Squirt?

Wiping her hands on her apron she headed to the garage, determined to make Squirt take over. She was tired, and had a hell of a headache building behind her left eye. It would help if she could get more than two hours of sleep a night.

Making her way across the compound, she entered the garage through the wide open bay doors. This can't be good. It never was when the doors were open. Usually the two of them tried to hide their extracurricular activities, or hobbies as Razor preferred to call them, but when Squirt was willing to be all in the open, it meant she was deep in her head working to solve a problem and M.J. had a cold chance in hell of convincing her to lend a hand.

Whose brilliant idea had it been to come here? Oh yeah, hers.

Stupid, M.J.

"But how did you improve the efficiency?"

"I rerouted the feedback to make the oxygen flow faster."

"Squirt?"

Two heads popped out from beneath the car. Squirt jumped out of the pit first, and then Bobby followed. "Hey M.J., long time no see."

She gazed uneasily at the man she once knew in a group home, the same center of neglect Squirt's mom had saved her from. He still had the long brown hair, hanging down in his face. As a child his features were so fine, he was almost pretty, which she guessed he'd still be called. To her, she noticed his eyes were narrowed and had a hard gleam in them, his lips were thin, as if he rarely smiled, and his nose was now twisted from having been broken more than once. "Bobby. Good to see you, I've heard you really made a name for yourself on the circuit."

"I try my best, but I was just telling your little Squirt that the real money is in engines."

"M.J., Bobby says he can get me the rest of the pieces I need—"

"In exchange for what?"

"Hey, M.J., I just want to help a sister out."

"My sister, Bobby, and you're forgetting how well I know you. Now, what do you want in exchange for the pieces?"

"I was thinking she'd want to share credit, that's all."

"Share credit?" Squirt whirled on Bobby. "What does that mean?"

"You just said you couldn't do it without my help, so it only seems fair to give up part of the control. Come on, Squirt." M.J. watched with a little bit of horror and a whole lot of humor as Bobby tried to wink at Squirt.

Who wrinkled her nose. "I think something's wrong with your eye."

M.J. didn't even try to stop the laugh that came bubbling out of her. "Bobby, give it up. Squirt doesn't share her toys, and she shouldn't have to. Now, the drivers have their own bunkhouse, and the teams have assigned engineering bays. In other words, go back to your own area. We have work to do."

He stared at her for a moment, eyes narrowed, and M.J. wished so hard that one of the Clan Lords would show up, she felt something in her middle lurch violently. Out of the corner of her eye, she thought she caught sight of a guy dressed in gold robes, but shaking her head, she reminded herself she barely slept anymore from wanting Aquos so much, or crying for him. Bobby seemed to make up his mind about something. He held up his hands in surrender, and backed away from Squirt. "I get it. No problem. Squirt, I'll make sure to catch you later."

She stayed still as he strutted out of the garage. There was no way in hell she was going to let anyone hurt Squirt. Even if she didn't love her with her entire being, she owed it to her mom for saving her.

"When you warned me that some of the drivers were dicks on the outside as well as on the inside, you meant guys like him, huh?"

"Yes, Squirt," she smiled. "Bobby is a big dick on the inside."

"What about the outside?"

"I knew him when he was ten years old, Squirt. I imagine it's grown."

"What if it didn't?"

"That would explain why he's in such a bad mood," M.J. said.

"So when you told him there was work to do you really just said it to make him go away, right?"

M.J. stared at her with one eyebrow raised.

"Please?"

"I've already done most of it."

"But remember, I covered for you while you were off sleeping with all those guys."

"There was one guy, Squirt. Just one. The rest were just friends."

"Come on, M.J.—"

"Stop complaining and do the right thing, Squirt."

"But, I'm so good at complaining."

M.J. continued to stare at Squirt, waiting for her to do the right thing.

"I really want to see what I can do without Bobby's parts, so I won't be tempted."

Folding her arms over her chest, she rocked from toe-to-heel waiting.

"Pretty please, M.J.?"

"Get your damned ass in the kitchen."

M.J. chuckled as Squirt dragged her feet and made the most dramatic path she could out of the garage toward the snack kitchen. She might not want to volunteer for the work, but once it was in front of her, she knew Squirt would roll up her sleeves and soon be happily rolling pretzels until they were done. Sitting down for a moment, she felt as if her head weighed a hundred pounds, it seemed so heavy. Sleeping for eight hours was a distant memory. Her eyes drifted shut for a moment, and instantly, all she could see was Aquos. His short black hair, his dark brooding eyes, and that stubble that outlined his jaw and cleft chin, so perfect for her to rub her cheek against.

Fuck, she missed him.

Remembering the never-ending Razor to-do list, she dragged herself up from the bench and started to close the bay doors and lock up. If Bobby was sniffing around Squirt's stuff, there was no way in hell she was going to make it easy for him to steal. Foster kids always knew how to get their mitts on crap they shouldn't, though most of the time it was stuff they needed. Like food. One time it was blankets and socks, during an especially brutal winter.

"Nice to see you taking care of my home."

Crap. Razor. What fresh hell is this?

"Hey Razor, good to see you. We're almost done with the pretzels."

"You are a piss poor excuse for a janitor."

"Razor, Squirt and I are your janitors, your catering prep, your maintenance and landscaping crew. We do all of those jobs, and you haven't managed to pay us in months. So do me a favor and shove your job review up your ass."

"I can kick you out, you know, right on your ass."

"Go ahead," she yelled, no longer able to care. "And stop talking about my damn fine ass!"

Tearing back to the kitchen, she froze in the shadow of the snack stand. In the distance she could see Bobby, meeting with three tall men dressed in fancy suits. They handed him something which he threw on the floor. When he leaned over, she made out the glint of something silver stuck in the back of his pants.

A gun. Had to be, right?

It looked like Squirt hadn't been being dramatic when she claimed she saw men with guns prowling around the track. What was Bobby up to? She watched uneasily as Razor joined the four men and rushed them out of view.

Like it wasn't dangerous enough already.

Tears flooded her eyes. Where are you Aquos? The man of her dreams was real, he just wasn't here, and she was beginning to fear she might be dead before he figured out he needed to get over himself and beg her to come back.

41

Squirt unfolded the quilt and draped it over M.J. as she slept on the couch. Her foster sister was beautiful. She brushed a streak of flour from her cheek and smiled when she grimaced. When her mother had gotten sick, she warned Squirt about M.J.'s true nature. *She needs someone to take care of,* Mom told her. *Make sure she always has someone who needs her.* So Squirt had tried to be that person for the only family she had left. At first it was easy, because she did need M.J. Her Mom had died of cancer when she was sixteen, and everything was a mess. No money. No place to live. No one to help.

But they had each other.

Eventually Squirt got better, but M.J. still seemed to need her, so she continued as she was. Things were different now, though. M.J. needed someone else beside her, and she didn't know what to do.

The guy with the dark hair and darker eyes was clearly M.J.'s. His eyes never left her face when they were together, and he kept reaching out to her as if he couldn't stand for them not to be connected. She didn't get who would name their kid 'Aquos' but maybe it was like Squirt, a beloved nickname from childhood one refused to give up, no matter how old.

Going outside, she looked around as she opened the garage, and froze.

Why the hell was there some guy wandering around the track dressed in a sheet?

Maybe not a sheet, but whoever that was, no way he was a driver. He wore gold colored fabric, which was draped around him in multiple ways. And, tilting her head, she could vaguely make out the hilt of a sword sticking up over his shoulder. M.J. had been bugging Razor about getting some security. It made sense that the cheapskate had hired guys fired by some Renaissance Faire.

But still. Robes? What century did he think it was?

* * *

Tamar closed the book he had been reading and returned it to the shelf. Gazing at the library, his brow furrowed as he considered the sheer untouched quality about the room. Sure, everything was spotless clean. But where were the indentations in the cushions from the many asses that had spent their time reading through the night?

He approved of this room, even if it wasn't designed for dragonkind. There were dozens of different kinds and styles of lamps around comfortable seating so one could pick a spot that suited one's needs and eyes best. The shelves were dark wood, gleaming with oil polish; there were large windows to fill the main area with natural light, but didn't reach the precious books, to prevent fading of the leather bindings. There were even cases with glass doors to doubly insure the safety of the precious remnants of their civilization from dust or microbe.

So where were the Clan Lords?

How could they enter their future without understanding the past?

Tamar felt old. Too old. He didn't understand the Clan Lord's fascination with this technology they loved so much. The large piece of glass they enjoyed convening around to witness these sporting events they favored, or something called adventure movies, escaped him. Forget the gaming they also tried to intrigue him with. What fun was it to vanquish enemies when you were not allowed to enjoy eating them afterward? There was no smell of blood, no roars of other dragonkind, no burn in your muscles as you labored through the day to end a battle.

It was all so empty to him.

Like the library was empty.

Speaking of which, he'd summoned elementals many hours ago and yet none had come. Which boded more ill for the Clan Lords than they realized.

The elementals were the start of the clans. They were the very bedrock Omegicon had been built upon. If they were ill or even, Oracle forbid, dying, the Clan Lords would not survive for long. And there was no way he was going to allow them to take sanctuary to the limbolands.

Looking around again, he made his way to the entrance.

The clan scrolls were not in the library. The clan history was also missing.

The elementals controlled and maintained the library.

And the elementals were missing.

No way this could add up to anything else than what he suspected.

So the question was … what was he going to do about it?

His priority was, and would always be, dragonkind. But his Queen, the one who had resurrected his entire race, seemed to cherish the rest of the clans with equal fervor. She even insisted on staying mated to Drake, the traitor. So if his priority was dragonkind, and Queen Salvation treated all of the Clan Lords as dragon, it meant he had to have loyalty to everyone.

Tamar hated that idea with every fiber of his being.

Dragonkind had always taken care of itself, recognizing that the other clans saw them as little more than a prize to hang on their walls. But the isolation of the past had led them all to the brink of extinction. If the Oracle and her Dioscuri had not interfered, they would not have lasted for long.

Which meant he was going to have to share what he suspected with the others.

He was just determined to make sure he did not say a word until he was positive it would benefit his people the most.

* * *

Stealth and Blade found Mach sitting in the clearing with a brass bell lying by his side. "Hey, little brother," Blade said.

"What's with the bell?"

"I keep trying to use it to call Turbo back," Mach answered. He didn't get up or even look at the two Clan Lords as they knelt on either side of him. "It should work. It always works. We can't resist the sound."

"But he doesn't come."

"No," Mach said to Blade.

"You can't make Turbo do anything he doesn't want to."

Mach shook his head, "It should have worked, Stealth. I don't know what or who he is anymore. He's so angry all the time. That's not Turbo."

"He's been different since the accident," Blade said.

"Yeah, Sally brought him back, but I lost him anyway."

"Mach, give him some time, little brother. You never know. Maybe he just needs to find his way back on his own."

"He's lost in the dark, Stealth. You know better than anyone the only way to find your path in the dark is if someone shines some fucking light." He chucked the bell into the woods. "And there's no fucking light for any of us anymore."

* * *

"Food again, Sally-mine?" When his wife whirled around with a fried chicken leg in her left hand, the blueberry bowl in her right and a smear of peanut butter across her lips, he laughed. "I see it is." He licked the peanut butter from her lips and gave her a deep kiss, while he was there. "Delicious," Drake said before taking a bite of the chicken. He moved back fast before she threw it at him. "And spicy."

"Get your own."

"Not to mention testy. What ails my mate?" Sally continued to stare at the chicken, which was now on the floor. "Sweet? What is it?"

"That was the last one."

"Ask the elementals to get another."

"I can't," she hiccupped. Drake's eyes were horrified as they watched the tears suddenly stream down her face. "There is no more."

"Sally," he tenderly drew her close to his chest. "There's always more."

"No, there's not," she sobbed. "And this is the last bowl of blueberries. I've been trying to make them last, but it's so hard."

"I know," he patted her back. "Blueberries are your kryptonite."

"Opposite of kryptonite," Sally said between sobs. "Drake, I don't know what to do. The elementals are all missing. None of them respond to our requests. I keep sending poor Hunter to get takeout, but everyone here eats like horses. He's maxed out four credit cards already. And …"

Drake waited, continuing to rub her back while she sobbed uncontrollably. He felt so useless. His way was to fight or kill. Either he would gladly do if it would get his female to stop crying, but right now, it sounded like the world had ended for her and no one had told him. He knew he had to be patient with a pregnant female, so he kept rubbing her back and letting her soak his shirt. He could get more shirts, though he did notice the other day that his closet was getting decidedly empty. The elementals always handled the laundry and putting stuff away.

How Sally was managing to keep the kitchen this clean was probably a miracle.

"Tell me, my love. Tell me what's making you cry so?"

"Blueberry bushes," she gasped out.

"What about the blueberry bushes?"

"I went to the green house to get more, but they're empty. No one's been tending it and everything is all overgrown and dying."

"Seriously?"

When she nodded with her eyes shining from the tears leaking from the corners, her nose red from her sobs, and lips trembling, Drake realized this was no time for patience. Blueberries were what was keeping his female happy while she grew their son. Blueberries were what kept her dragonself in stasis so the babe could be healthy and grow to full term.

Blueberries were also her favorite snack after sex.

He roared as he set her gently to the side and went running to find

Luke. It was time for the Light Clan leader to man the fuck up and take control. There was no way his Sally was going to spend one more moment weeping, and Luke would have to be the one who fixed things.

42

Aquos felt like everything was broken. Bones, heart, spirit and mind. He had never felt so healthy, and yet was unable to manage to accomplish a damned thing. All he really wanted to do was sit in his hot tub and dream about his girl. M.J.'s miracle dust seemed to have cured them. The Omegicon were used to lightning storms, so maybe there was some part of this fulgurite, as she called it, in their atmosphere. Regardless. The great pans of dust in each of their chambers seemed to be enough to tip the scales in their favor.

For the first time in decades, all of them were physically fit.

Even Luke, the first to grow ill and the one to feel it the most, was seen running through the forest with a pack over his shoulders and a lantern in hand. He was clearly determined to find something, but Aquos didn't bother asking him what. Unless it was M.J., he honestly didn't give a shit what their fearless leader was setting out to find. All he wanted was his girl back.

He was floating in the hot tub, trying to use the warmth to lighten the cold gripping his heart, when Luke returned. "I want you to come with me."

"Sally told me about the boy scouts, but aren't you a little old?"

"Ancient, Aquos. I'm a fucking ancient. I still think you want to come with me."

"I'll pass. When I float in here I can just about make out M.J.'s eyes in the stars."

"And here I thought you'd like a shot at getting your girl back."

Aquos jumped out of the water, instantly drying. "Where we going?"

"To the library."

He stared at Luke's retreating back. "What the fuck happens in the library?"

Following Luke, the two of them were soon inside the library with the doors closed. Aquos looked around, shocked. The room was leather, shiny wood, big chairs with comfortable cushions and pools of colored lights from stained glass. It looked, for all intents and purposes, like something straight out of a magazine.

And used about as much.

"What the fuck happens in a library?"

"Me. I love libraries, and your Son of Light prefers to meet me here."

"Well met, archangel," Luke bowed, so Aquos followed suit.

"Bowing is not required, gentle lords, unless it is your preference. Rise, Luke and Aquos, and explain to me why is it that the compact clearly states you will stay within the boundaries of Sanctuary's grounds, and yet, your people appear to be running amok through the Pennsylvanian countryside."

"That's not why we are here," Luke sputtered.

"Who is running amok?" Aquos smiled at the idea of any of the Clan Lords hearing that description.

Drake came barging in, "Luke we need to discuss the elementals."

Mach, Stealth and Blade followed, with an equal amount of flush to their faces. "Luke, we need to decide what to do about Turbo. And where are the elementals? Our rooms are almost destroyed." Stealth said.

Blade nodded. "You don't know how big of a pig you are until someone stops cleaning after you."

"Apparently I'm a slob." Mach spoke with such blatant shock, the others smiled.

Tamar and Hunter were the last to join the throng, "Luke, there is something you needs know about the elementals."

Aquos held up one finger, "Is it that they're running amok?"

"Bingo," Gabrielle clapped at his guess and the other lords' glowers.

"What is it about the elementals?"

"They've left," Drake said.

Gabrielle shook her head. "Technically, they have gone home."

"Excuse you?"

Tamar stepped in front of the snorting Blade, eyeing Gabrielle. "I know you."

"Archangel Gabrielle is a guardian for this world's residents."

"No," Tamar said. "She is Dioscuri."

Luke pushed Tamar back, grunting when the big man didn't even flinch at the shove. "She is not maiden beholden to my mother's will. Archangel Gabrielle is the protector for the Earthers and our primary intermediary for the compact."

"This being is Dioscuri, son of the Oracle. I know of what I speak."

Aquos realized this was not going to end well if someone didn't step up. Everyone else appeared just happy to sit back and let the dragon rip Luke and Gabrielle apart. He knew someone who was calm needed to speak. Since he had no heart anymore, it might as well be him. "Gabrielle, are you from our world?"

"I am both," she demurred. "The Omega and the Alpha were made by the same creature. My function was to guard and inspire both. Who do you think has always argued on your behalf with the others? Why would I do such a thing, jeopardizing all that is here and puts itself in harm's way, even with our constant watch? Did you think you were less loved by the creator? I am here for them. I am here for you. I am. Everywhere and at all times. As it should be."

"What is it you came to tell us? Something about the elementals?"

"Your elementals are gone from Sanctuary's grounds. You should have an interest in such things."

"But I think I know why they left," Tamar stated.

Aquos didn't care about such things. "What about M.J.? If you're from Omega, perhaps you know which clan she belongs to?"

"I thought it was clear. Sally claimed her as dragon. You own her heart. The speedsters owe her a debt of honor, and Light Clan ... well, I believe Light Clan must feel a certain amount of indebtedness to her as well, no?"

"Yes," Luke said. He smiled so wide, even Aquos had to admit he was a good-looking fucker. "Definitely. Light Clan owes M.J. as well."

"So why are you concerned over M.J.'s clan of hailing?" Tamar asked Aquos.

Everyone's heads did the swivel thing to stare him down. Hells. Like he wanted to be the center of attention when he wasn't feeling the archangel's fiery eyes. "I just ... see on Omega, Water Clan wasn't revered."

"A fallacy taught to you by your sire," Blade said.

"One we would all appreciate you dropping," Stealth added.

"You are my best friend, but in this I cannot agree." Drake said. "Even in my earliest memories I recalled the Water Clan being the key to our survival. The blight attacked themfirst, for it knew that destroying water would take the world."

Aquos sighed, trying to believe what Drake was saying.

"You are water," Gabrielle shrugged. "M.J. is who she is. But she could not love you more, no matter from whence you hail."

"Luke would never let her live here."

"Is that why you broke up with her?" Luke's incredulous expression made the other's snort when Aquos sheepishly nodded. "Aquos, Gabrielle already told us she was Omega. I could never refuse her entry to these halls for fear of breaking the compact. You know how serious I take the rules."

"And her foster sister? Because Luke, I saw how she was with that girl. M.J. would never leave someone she cared for."

"Which should tell you all you need to know about her clan."

Gabriellele's words did little to clear the confusion he was feeling, though it did seriously make him reconsider stopping Drake and Luke from ripping each other, and the archangel, or Dioscuri, into pieces. "So she's Light?"

"I think I'd remember a sister," Luke stated baldly.

"Your M.J. is not of the Light, though her people were older. I'll say no more, other than the girl known as Squirt may also live in this place if it is the Clan Lords wish. Her involvement with the one you call M.J. is too tight to separate the strands of their fates at this point, and I feel she may have some of the clues for which you seek."

Mach chuckled. "I'd love Squirt to move in. Did you see her garage?"

"I, as well, feel M.J.'s Squirt would make an interesting change to our hall."

Stealth rolled his eyes. "Blade's got a crush on the young one."

"Who doesn't?" Mach added.

"Underneath all the oil and grime, young Squirt does make an intriguing female, indeed." Hunter's smile turned from his normal friendly to an oily ooze. He purposefully avoided the shocked gaze of Tamar.

"Watch yourself, lizard boy," Blade tightened his hand on the hilt of his sword.

"M.J. is Aquos', and Squirt belongs to him."

"In other words," Stealth filled in for Blade, "hands off."

"They really have no idea what I'm like," Hunter muttered to Tamar.

Drake put his hands on his hips. "Nor will they, as long as you dwell in Sanctuary. It's decided. M.J., no matter what clan she was born to, is dragonkind now, so she belongs here. Thus, her foster sister belongs here as well. The only question is, who among us is going to tell her?"

He ran, yes ran, through Sanctuary, determined to get to the cars first. Aquos didn't care that Mach could drive faster, or the dragons could fly it, or even Luke could transport him there with a blink of his eyes. He wanted - no needed - to do it, and he needed to do it right now.

Skidding to a stop he realized he had no idea which vehicle to take. Aquos kept thinking about M.J., living in that pit working her fingers until they were raw. Just her and a young girl, the only ones to keep that entire facility going.

It was insane and needed to be stopped right now.

He stepped into a puddle, leftover from the last hard rain, and used the water to transfer his mind's eye to the track. While he waited for one of the guys to join him and help, it was solely his intention to see how M.J. and

Squirt were doing. To check they were alone and able to start packing so they could finally come here. Surely the agony he felt every day would dissipate if he knew she was close.

The water convened with a rain barrel outside the garage.

M.J. She was standing outside, and looked tired. Beautiful, but tired. Her hair held back by a dirty red cloth, she wore a faded gray pair of coveralls , with a pail of tools in her hands. A human male stood in front of her. He was handsome, dressed in a pristine white shirt, slacks with a crisp crease someone had pressed for him, and a pair of shiny shoes.

Aquos hated him on sight, or on water vision.

For he also noticed that in the man's hands he carried a bouquet of flowers. The roses were visible in his meager sight from the rain barrel drops dripping down the side. He'd never given M.J. flowers. He'd never given her anything but someone to take care of, and problems, and the never-ending feuding of the Clan Lords.

Suddenly, the last thing Aquos wanted to do was tell M.J. anything at all.

43

"Roses? Seriously Bobby? You got Squirt, roses? Have you met my sister?" M.J. couldn't stop the giggles at the idea of her tomboy sibling having the first clue as to what to do with a bunch of delicate roses. They weren't even the good kind of roses, the ones that were long stemmed. These were the ones with the short stems you usually got outside of the Stop and Shop.

"Look M.J., just because you're a man-eating bitch doesn't mean your little, and might I add, much hotter, sister has to be."

Once upon a time, Bobby's dig would have hurt her. Deeply.

But Bobby was a pale, small little man compared to her Aquos. Bobby could barely figure out how to shine his own shoes. Aquos commanded all water if he wanted, inside their bodies and on the planet.

Let him throw shade. She knew how to be her own sun.

"You can call me all the names you want to Bobby. It isn't going to make Squirt like a bunch of flowers, or change her mind about her engine. And it is her engine. It may have us eating ramen every day for six years, but I made sure she had a great patent attorney to protect Squirt's intellectual property at each step of her process. Don't even think of pulling one of your moves on her."

His fingers wrapped as tight as a vise around her upper arm, making her wince. "You little bitch. I'm the one Squirt's mom should have adopted. Why she wanted a little gutter shadow like you—"

"Go home, Bobby. Nobody wants you here. Nobody ever did."

Bobby looked behind her at Squirt, who stood in the doorway to the garage with a large wrench in her hands, as if it were a bat. Bobby was about to learn just what Squirt could do with that wrench, and where their mother taught them to aim when dealing with guys like him. He spat at M.J., hitting her squarely on the cheek, but only because she turned her head in time.

He threw the flowers to the ground.

Squirt came over to stand next to M.J., watching him stomp away. She glanced at the flowers, confused. "What did he think I'd do with those?"

"No idea."

"He was wrong, you know."

"About what?"

"Momma was never going to adopt him. She said there was something in the eyes of the other kids in that home. They'd all gone hard and dark. Yours still had light. Hope. She could see your potential even when you were just entering your teens. She knew you wanted a home as much as you needed it. She knew you'd make a great sister, and you have."

"Thank you, Squirt."

"Now it's time to do something for you. I vote we play hooky. Razor is distracted with the big event, and the track is all ready. Let's go down to your beach and see if we can't find any more of those glass things. You can make more dust for those hunky guys and have them pick it up with a big case of delicious food again."

"I didn't know you noticed guys on that level, Squirt."

She laughed. "Of course I do. Those guys are way too big not to notice, M.J. Besides, they come with a cooler of food. Enough to last us a week and a half."

"Good point. I'll race you to the car."

Within a half an hour, they were in the track's sedan that Razor used to transport the drivers if they flew in for an event. Squirt managed to pack up what was left from the dragon's delivery and stock the back seat. She had retrieved her pail of tools, including the packing box she preferred to transport the fulgurite when she dug it out of the smoking sands.

It took three hours to make it to the small resort town in Delaware where she'd found she'd get the best results. Squirt set up the food on a picnic table and positioned the tent over it. They sat and ate in comfortable silence, their ears still ringing from the music they blared over the long drive. M.J. had always thought the best part of having a family would be all the talking. She was shocked to discover the parts she loved the most were that you could sit with family in comforting silence, just knowing all the other person needed to know was you were there. Squirt pulled out her most recent project's blueprints and became lost in her configurations.

Her sister never asked her about Aquos or what she was planning to do. Maybe she didn't have to. It wasn't like she couldn't hear her cry all night long.

M.J. turned to the horizon and watched the building storm. The little resort town had long since seen its zenith. The motels lining the beach were built in the 1950s at best; their faded exteriors made her think of a line of little old ladies, their makeup long since past its use by date. She imagined on a sunny day this might be the spot for the aging population to come and sit and enjoy the sun. She only came here when it was about to rain. There had to be people in the buildings, but few would venture out when the sky turned into smoke, and the clouds made it feel as if God had lowered the ceiling of the world to punish us for some reason.

Glancing at Squirt she noticed her sister was doodling … what looked like an elemental. "Who is that?"

"Some security guard Razor hired, I think," Squirt shrugged.

Three large dark SUVs squealed into the parking spaces near them. Out of the cars came a small army of men in dark shirts, and Bobby. *Crap. This couldn't be good.* "We have company." Squirt didn't respond, and knowing her sister too well, she got that her message had not been received. So she did the only thing a big sister could. She flicked her ear until Squirt looked up at her, blinking. "Company, Squirt. The bad kind."

"When is company ever a good thing?"

M.J. smiled at their Mom's favorite quote. "Bobby. What a surprise. I didn't know you liked the beach. And you brought friends."

"We don't want trouble," Bobby said. He nodded to his friends, who surrounded M.J. and Squirt. One of his suited companions made a point of moving his jacket so they could clearly see the gun in his belt. "These guys are here to make you see reason. Sign over the patents, Squirt, give me all the blueprints, and no one has to get hurt. I promise you."

"I haven't even finished testing it yet."

"Doesn't matter. We want it."

"How come?"

"I'm not explaining myself to an idiot girl."

"An idiot girl whom you have to steal from."

Bobby took a step toward M.J. with his fists clenched. "This isn't about you, bitch. I'm talking to her."

Squirt jumped in front of her, and M.J. pushed her back behind her, which started a shoving match between the two of them until one of the suited men drew a gun and aimed it at both of them. "No," Bobby yelled. "I checked with the lawyer, we need the girl to sign the paperwork and take her blueprints."

"I don't understand why you want an engine I haven't finished perfecting."

M.J. tried to resist the urge to smack Squirt. *What did it matter?* They were threatening them with guns. "They're going to use it to rig races," she guessed. "Not the point, Squirt."

"Of course it is." Turning to M.J. she tilted her head. "Didn't you see that weird security guard? We need to stall until he can get help."

44

Aquos still knelt by the puddle in the driveway while his heart continued to reel from what he'd seen. He'd been here for hours. He'd felt the passing of the sun in the surface temperature of the water. There was no reason to have his eyes open. They were still closed, desperately trying to erase the mental torture he'd just willingly subjected himself to. M.J. was the kindest, most caring female he'd ever met. It was no surprise someone else wanted her as much as he did. His head fell forward, regretting that he hadn't take the time to bind her to him in as many ways as he could. He hadn't want to rush her. He worried she needed time.

He was a fucking idiot.

Drake was clearly determined to give him plenty of time to adjust to his approach, based on the amount of noise the dragon made as he slowly came closer. Why would he run away? There was no longer anywhere to run to or any reason to bother trying. He would happily sit here until this world ended as well. "Whats up, my brother?"

"You've been spending too much time with Mach."

Aquos shrugged. "We're both heart sore. Might as well."

"Misery doesn't love company; it loves solutions."

"Says the guy who lived in a tower most of the time before he found his girl."

"And you found yours, so why the fuck are you sitting here?" Drake folded his arms over his chest.

"What's the matter, dragon. Worried I'll start pining for your girl, again?"

"Nope." Drake perched on the edge of the fountain the elementals had drained on the last day of summer, stretched out his legs, and balanced one foot on top of the other, as if it were the most important act in the history of their people. Aquos knew he was searching for the right words, but he was taken aback by the ones that came out of his mouth. "You love me. It made sense you'd love Sally as well. I was the first one to notice how fast you dropped that crush as soon as you met M.J."

"So what's with the interrogation?"

"Enquiring minds want to know."

"Bullshit."

"No. It's not. We're here for you, Aquos, but, no offense, you're acting like an ass."

"She's found someone else, Drake."

"I don't believe that for a second."

"Well, I saw it. With my own eyes!"

Drake snorted at his pain and outrage. "Aquos, you are one of the smartest males I know. I have no idea what you think you just saw, but I know you're wrong. I saw the way she looked at you. Fuck, we all did. M.J. Storm is head-over-heels for you, buddy. And you can sit here all you want to, but when it comes down to it, you two are meant to be together."

"I can't believe you're being such a dick—"

"Ditto, asshole."

"She's moved on, Drake. He brings her flowers."

He laughed at him. Drake threw back his head and laughed, long, loud belly laughs that felt like they went on for days. Aquos would have attacked him, but he knew it wiser not to tackle a dragon.

"I really hate you right now." Aquos' eyes narrowed as Drake wiped his streaming eyes.

"No. No you don't. I suspect you think you hate a great many aspects of the last few hours, but I'm not one of them. You're forgetting something, though."

"What?"

"M.J. is Omega. She's got to come live here, no matter what. So go ahead and think she's found someone else. I give her about twenty minutes before she just knocks you down and tries to suffocate you with kisses."

He smiled at the image and the memory of M.J.'s belief she'd raped him. As if.

"You are also forgetting the true nature of your girl. I'm thinking you could bring her a lot of gifts. Stuff for her artwork. Probably something for that kid sister of hers that she adores. But do you really think a girl like M.J. gives a crap about flowers? Flowers, Aquos, really? I thought you had more sense than that. I damn well know M.J. does."

Aquos scowled as he considered Drake's words. He was right. He could see M.J. wanting any number of gifts. Flowers wouldn't be first on his list. Or, he imagined, M.J.'s. He stood up, his hands opening and closed against his thighs as if he were already reaching out to hold her.

"What's the deal? Should we take the van and the Rover to make sure we've got enough room to pack their shit up?"

Looking at Mach, Blade and Stealth, all eager to go and help him, Aquos recognized that one way or another, M.J. was coming to live in this house. It was up to him to do everything he could to make sure when she did, she wanted to live in his wing instead of the weird empty wing the elementals claimed they required when they built the place. "Throw some boxes in, too."

"There's my friend." Drake glowed with happiness at Aquos' decision, even if it was only implied.

"It's about fucking time," Stealth muttered.

A flash of light went off and one of the gold elementals appeared in front of them. He could hear the other Clan Lords curse their surprise. The elemental looked around and frowned. "Not enough." He snapped his fingers, and Aquos almost fell over when all the other Clan Lords appeared, as well as Tamar. "Still not enough." The elemental waved his hand again and they heard the roar of an animal in the distance.

"Excuse you," Sally screeched. Her hair was rumpled and her favorite throw blanket was clutched in her hands, as if she'd just been bodily dragged out of her bed from a really good nap.

Drake rushed over to Sally, while Hunter and Tamar moved to flank their queen as if she were under attack. All three dragons eyed the elemental with suspicion. "When did you get powers?"

The elemental ignored Drake's snarled question. "Danger."

"Where the hell have you been?"

Luke's query was met with equal silence. "Danger. She and the young one are in danger," the elemental repeated.

M.J. It had to be M.J. "Can you take us to her?"

"I want to go."

"No," Drake refused his wife.

"She's my friend, and my people."

"There is no way in hell I'm letting an elemental do some type of poofing thing with you when you are growing our son."

"You get points for the 'our son' part," Sally said.

"When did you get powers?" Luke asked the elemental.

Aquos rolled his eyes as Luke continued to sputter. "What the fuck does that matter right now? M.J. is in danger."

"Tell us where to go and we'll follow." Drake transformed into his dragonself, with Hunter and Tamar following. "Show us the location in your mind, we'll be a few seconds behind, but will follow. Good. His M.J.

deserved an army to defend his girl, and three dragons were one hell of an army. Sally used Drake's wing and leg to catapult onto his back, where she looked at home.

"M.J. is dragonkind. Nobody messes with my clan."

"We regained our powers when she returned to us," the elemental answered Luke. "Now we must go. All of you."

The bellow of the same outraged animal reached them again.

"Just take me to her," he ordered.

"Us, too," Stealth, Blade, Mach and Luke chorused. For the first time in what felt like days, Aquos truly smiled. The Clan Lords were once more united, along with three dragons and one very pissed off and pregnant queen. The last time they were like this some mercenaries had attacked Sanctuary but soon became convinced all the money in the world wasn't worth taking on the Omegicon.

Whatever was threatening his female was about to meet a very messy end.

He almost pitied the fool threatening her.

45

The suited men and Bobby had made them back up onto the beach until they were out of the immediate view of the motel windows. They seemed to be having an argument over the best way to kill them and still get the paperwork done. Modern day mobsters. More scared of lawyers than they were of the actual police. M.J. stood on the edge of the surf, the waves soaking her shoes, as she watched the storm build at sea. The clouds were dark as smoke, roiling over each other. They looked angry, as if they had a beef with the guys holding the guns on her and Squirt, and they were determined to take care of things.

She'd seen storms here plenty of times. This one was different.

Thunder was the next thing she noticed. Not individual booms. They came fast. One after another as if they were racing each other. The air changed. It grew thick and heavy, pressing in on her skin, making her t-shirt and jeans stick to her skin. Something was happening.

Something bad.

What a shame. She really wanted to see Aquos before she died. If for no other reason than to kick him in the shins for walking away from what they had.

"M.J.?"

"This is what the end of the world looks like."

Squirt glanced at her as if she'd officially lost her mind. Why not? Her heart and soul had left a long time before, about the moment that Aquos stepped away from her in the garage. "They're going to kill us," Squirt trembled underneath the arm she had around her shoulders. "I thought the security guy would help."

"It'll be okay, Squirt."

"No, it won't."

"Yes, it will."

"How do you know?"

"I won't let it be anything else." She pushed her foster sister behind her and stepped closer to the thugs. This was her shot. It was time to pay back Squirt's family for everything they'd done for her. Squirt was going to go home, and live a long full life. M.J. didn't care anymore about her own future.

She was tired. Bone deep tired in a way that felt all the rest in the world would never change things.

Life wasn't worth it without her goth-boy.

"Gentlemen, you've been sadly misinformed. Squirt's invention isn't available. It won't help you rig races, or anything else for that matter. We're done with you, and you would be better served to forget we exist."

"We want the engine, damn it. She gives it to us, or we kill her."

"No!"

In a flash of light she saw Aquos, Luke and the rest of the Clan Lords arrive, a little behind the gun-wielding idiots facing off with her. They thought this was a gun fight, when it had now become a superhero battle. The looks on the Omegicon guys' faces were clear to her. They were here to kill these idiots. She couldn't allow Aquos to do that. The death of his father was still a shadow darkening his soul.

There was no way she would let her safety take any of his light.

"Put your guns down," she screamed at the thugs, honestly trying to save their lives. "All of you, put those things away now. Bobby, we grew up together. You can't do this to us. You know Squirt, you loved her Mom, just as much as I did. Please, you can't do this. You can't be this guy. Don't do this. Don't make me watch you die."

"You were always an egotistical bitch."

He snatched a gun from the man next to him, raised it to her head, and took aim.

Everything slowed down, as if she could see each millisecond in a vivid color photograph someone presented her to review. The lightning chose that moment to come. Flashes came, as fast as a sneezing attack, and as controlled. They lit the sky with their cold electric light. M.J. laughed, threw her head back and laughed as the bolts left the water and began to strike around them. She held Squirt close to her body so she wouldn't run into the line of the heaven's fire.

She knew. She knew deep in her bones that the lightning was going to end their would-be attackers.

And she did not care.

Pushing Squirt to the ground, she threw her arms over her head. *Yes. Come.* These fools think they can hurt me? They think they can take the life of the girl I adore? Do it. Teach them the cost for daring to harm her. Teach them where they belong in the scheme of the world.

She was M.J. Storm and they would pay dearly for their daring.

They would die.

Her smile was both threatening and pitying when she dropped her arms. The next flash of lightning split into six bolts at once, striking the thugs and Bobby where they stood, electrocuting them. The lightning kept coming, as if it wanted to make sure the job was complete. The humans fell, smoking, charred, no longer able to harm anyone.

M.J. looked up and saw Aquos staring at her. He'd run directly into the firestorm, determined to get to her. He wanted to protect her. How like her goth-boy. Why didn't he understand? The person who needed protection was him.

"I'm sorry," tears streamed down her face. "You were right. Better to recover from some hurt now than a lifetime later. Take care of Squirt for me." She stepped away from Squirt, held her hands up to the still churning heavens and took one last look at the man she loved. And then called down the lightning again.

This time, it was she who disappeared.

46

Aquos felt frozen where he stood. Every molecule in his body had turned to ice. What had just happened? Since when did M.J. have powers? And the level of power she had. By the Oracle, they should have called her Magnificent. He ran to the spot and touched the warm sand, trying to understand where she'd gone. Looking out at the frothing sea, he reached the energy that existed in the molecules of the water so key to the survival of this world. Nothing. He couldn't sense M.J. at all.

He held no dominion over the sky, but the sky was filled with water and for him it was all his to command.

"Give her back," Aquos roared. He punched his arms out to the waves, sending it flying backwards. The sky grew dark with storm clouds and screeching birds. "I command you to give her back," his eyes bulged as spittle flew from his mouth with the volume of his order. "Give her back right now."

"Uhm … Aquos? This is getting serious."

He ignored Luke, shaking off his restraining arm. "Give her back," he continued to bellow at the water.

The waves had moved into the distance. He began to pace back and forth on the beach as his eyes strained against the gray green water. "I have never asked for anything. I never complained when you took my sire. But I will not exist without her. Give her back to me, right now."

His friends cursed when they saw the water rise in a tidal wave rushing towards them. The small resort town was about to experience a flood of epic, almost Biblical proportions, and they could hear the cries of the humans who saw their own incoming doom.

Aquos did not care. "Give me back M.J., and make sure she's whole."

Omegicon lords and humans alike could do little but witness what was about to occur. Aquos held up his hands with his palms out to stop the waves where they were. The tidal wave was twenty feet tall, churning with ocean life, held in place by the force of his will alone. He stared up into the clouds above him and called out with all his fear, despair and devotion, to this one female who meant everything to him. Even the safety and the future of his people and the ones he lived in the midst of did not matter in comparison to what he felt right now.

For what was life without a heart or soul?

"Give her back to me."

Nothing. Once more, the universe turned its back on him, and left him with nothing but sorrow and regret.

Aquos's knees folded, his head fell forward against his chest, and the sobs came to take him. As his rage ran from him, the waters just imploded. There was a sprinkling of hapless fish flapping uselessly trying to find a way to breathe.

Why did they bother?

Why would anyone want to bother to fight to live?

M.J. was gone.

How in this horrible world could she be gone?

Sally's light floral scent heralded her arrival beside him before her hand squeezed his shoulder. "Aquos ... I am so sorry."

He leaned forward, his arms wrapped around his shaking body, as he desperately tried to keep his form from fracturing into pieces as broken as his heart. His head pressed into the wet sand and he thought of the elementals who were always bowing when M.J. walked into a room. Of course they did. She was all things magnificent. "She did it for me. She wouldn't let them hurt anyone, and she didn't want me to bear the weight of killing again. How can I live in a universe where she isn't? Why would I even try?"

"You've lived a lot longer without her than you did with her." Turbo's snarled comment made the other men gasp with surprise.

Aquos flicked his hand and he heard Turbo start to gurgle as his body filled with a never-ending stream of water. *Who the hell found him anyway?* Better he stayed lost, lost for all time, as lost as Aquos felt without M.J. The Speed Clan was about to experience the extent of the power of his people.

One less monster for the world to suffer.

I would have gladly slain all of your monsters, my M.J.

"Dude, quit it. You're killing him."

The eyes he turned on Mach were hollowed out. As gutted as his soul. "Why would I care if Turbo dies? He hurt, M.J. And now she's gone. Let him hurt for the rest of time, for all I care."

"You don't mean that," Drake shook his head at Aquos' confession.

"Fuck it," Aquos turned to finally look at the eldest of the Speed Clan. He went to wave the water from Turbo's body, and then shrugged. *Let the bastard drown.* He was done with this.

He was done with them all.

 47

She was floating. The air embraced her, the clouds were her bed, the sun a blanket, and the breeze as gentle and teasing as Aquos at his sexy finest. M.J. did not know anyone could feel this … cherished.

Not outside of her male's embrace.

M.J. finally understood words like joy … peace … love.

Below her it was chaos and pain. Endless suffocating darkness. Here she was free. Here she was finally everything she dreamed she could be. She was finally her art, the visions in her mind, in all ways necessary. It was fulfilling in a way no act had ever been before. Not pride in her foster mother's face, not the contentment in Squirt's hugs, not even in completion of the perfect piece in her art.

The only thing missing was … him.

He will be lost to you if you do not return. He will be lost to the world if you make the wrong choice, child.

Gabrielle. Her voice came on the wind that washed over her like the waves in Aquos's pond. "I don't want to talk to you." She turned over, determined to physically and mentally block the pushy archangel. *Honestly.* Couldn't she see she was busy enjoying this absolute blissful freedom?

Here I thought you were the great and mighty M.J. Storm.

"You don't know me."

I was there when you first drew breath. I was there when the soul that animated you took possession of this form. I was there when the moirai wove your destiny into the weave that is the cloak of the Omegicon's Oracle.

"You didn't know who I was when we met."

I knew you, child. I have always known you.

"Feh. Shut it, fancy angel. I don't want to hear you right now."

Her voice I may use, but Gabriellele I am not.

"It's awful down there."

The water Clan Lord is many things, but awful is not one.

"He is pretty awesome."

If you are done, if your toil is complete, child, then continue on your way. This world may drown from the sorrow of his grief, but it will rise again. But down there is a male whose heart has broken and will take most that live with him.

Should he pass, so too do my children, so too does my world.

"Damn pushy angel with its poetic brain voice," she muttered. Looking up, M.J called a rainbow to wrap around her enjoying the feeling of the refracted light through the water droplets in the air. This was who she was. A child of the air. Of light and color. Movement and life. This was who she had always dreamt of without realizing what it meant. This was the heart of every piece of artwork she had sweated and bled trying to create.

And this was exactly what she wanted to explain to Aquos.

If he could be best friends with the dragons of fire, he'd better be prepared to fully embrace the air.

She scowled to make it clear to the pushy fancy pants angel she wasn't pleased.

But they both knew she had to return.

M.J. knew she was meant to be with Aquos.

The bubbling laughter that trailed after her was just best ignored.

* * *

He was a dead man. A walking corpse. Just a bag of skin holding water and few starry elements leftover from the creation of the universe. No hope. No joy. No need for heartbeats or a soul. He was death.

Aquos could hear the Omega Clan Lords doing what they could to calm the locals. The flooding was minimal. One thing he could say for Turbo, his nasty mouth had turned his anger from the water toward his former friend. He could still hear him gurgling as the water ebbed and flowed through Turbo's respiratory system. Mach was trying to help, but once again, Turbo was being a dick.

Screw him. Let him drown.

He heard the others curse when the storm clouds above were pierced by a shaft of lightning. Thunder echoed all around them as the storm clouds sped to hover over their heads like a great and mighty shadow of doom. He turned his head to the sky, and realized for the first time that he was crying. Aquos didn't know he even had the ability to do so anymore.

"Kill me. I beg of you. Just kill me."

Once more, the heavens turned its back on him.

The lightning went off again, great flashes of columns of light bursting around him. He stayed where he was. Too weak from rage and grief to move. Forget actually reacting to the danger.

Perhaps this was his answer after all.

Electrocution from lightning sounded like the right way to go.

It reminded him of his girl.

Faster they came, the thunder echoing in his ears, his eyes blinded by the glaring flares. They seemed to be circling him. Aquos could see past the pen of bolts as Drake and Sally tried to lunge to get him. The sheer force of the electricity being emitted pushed them back. Drake ended up holding Sally as they were immobilized by the danger. All they could do was watch.

Still they came. Faster and faster.

The air burned his nose with the spent electrocarbons. The ground around him smoked with the channeling of electricity into its depths. Aquos could feel the air grow thick and heavy, pressing on him as a weight.

Another round of fast lightning bolts surrounding him and then …

She was there.

M.J. in the flesh. Standing with her hair waving in the air, a silver cloak covering her body, her lips in a slight smile. "Goth-boy," she greeted him with a breathy sigh before catapulting herself into his arms. Her arms wrapped around his neck and back. Her mouth on his, tongue inside his mouth tasting, returning the breath he was sure he would never recover. Her soft body melting into his hardened frame, reminding him of things like warmth. Comfort. Happiness.

M.J. was where she belonged, in his arms. And he was in his only true home. In her arms.

And once more … he lived.

48

Her goth-boy. Their kiss felt like a marriage as their souls united into one great force. His taste filled her senses, their lips branded, their breaths wove. It was … perfection. "Goth-boy. My goth-boy," M.J. managed to cup his face so she could take stock of what damage had happened while she was gone. "Why are you crying? Who should I kill?"

The other Clan Lords began to slap each other on their backs at her arrival.

Mach just stayed by Turbo's side, trying to keep him from drowning as he stood on dry land.

"No one." A wave of his hand freed Turbo from his curse and allowed him to take his first free breath. Aquos buried his face in her neck, banded his arms around her waist and whirled her around and around, joyful just to feel her in his arms once more. "You are never to leave my hold again."

"Same to you, buddy."

Flashes of light separated them, though Aquos kept his female in his arms. The beach became filled with elementals. More than he'd ever seen in one space before. Luke had called assembly over their years here and he'd never seen this many. The beach became a mosaic of colored robes as each appeared, dropped to their knees and leaned forward until their foreheads pressed into the damp sand. Squirt came to stand next to M.J. and pointed to one of the males in gold robes. "That's the security guard I mentioned."

"He's no security guard."

"M.J.," Aquos took a few steps away from his girl and his jaw dropped open when the elementals continued to stay directed at her. "I think they are bowing to you. I don't know why or how, but it's you, sweetheart."

"That's impossible."

"What'd you do? How'd you break all these people, M.J.?"

She ignored Squirt, which was technically the job of a big sister. "Luke, do you understand why they're doing this?"

"I don't know." Luke came to stand on her other side.

Tamar also approached and gave her a low bow. "Hail to the Lady M.J. Heir to the great Weather Clan. Maker of the seasons that gave us life and the elementals who make our lives worth living. You have been long lost to the turning of the wheel, your return is surely a return of our people's resurgence."

M.J. swallowed hard when each of the Clan Lords turned amazed expressions at Tamar's words, then reverently went to their knees as the dragon knight had. Sally bowed her head, her pregnant belly clearly not allowing her to try something as hazardous as kneeling in sand. Tears blurred her vision as even Aquos bent his knee and lowered his forehead to the sand.

"Super, M.J. You broke them, too."

"Please, all of you, Clan Lords and elementals alike, please rise."

The people before her immediately responded, the elementals rising with cheers. She swallowed back a sob when she saw Aquos was still kneeling, his forehead down. Putting her hand on his short dark hair, she bit her lip. "Goth-boy. Please don't ruin this. Don't try to leave me again."

"I would willingly serve you all my days."

"My only wish is that you love me, Aquos. That's all I ever needed."

"I could do naught else."

She wiped away her tears as her body shook with her held back sobs. "Then why the hell aren't you kissing me?"

"Glad to be of use." He exploded from the ground. His arms, like steel bands around her, his lips brutally hard and yet tenderly soft, his entire being drawing her in to knit them together tighter than any legal or religious service ever could. They were one. They were each other's everything.

They were all they would ever need again.

Their mouths fused together. And the rest of the world faded into nothing.

* * *

Aquos knew he should feel guilty. He really should. He'd left his friends, men he called brothers, on the stretch of beach to take care of clean-up. He didn't even ask if they wanted help. Instead, having M.J. back in his arms, he ignored the world. They were transported back to their wing at Sanctuary and shut the door of their suite. Thanks to the elementals, they were kept with a never-ending stream of food and drink. It could have been months since they left.

Cuddling M.J. close to his side, he looked back down the hall toward their rooms in the dragon wing with regret. "I vote we take over the dragon's underground spring again and practice powers."

"We are not hiding in rooms anymore. I want to get to know my family."

"My M.J. ... are you sure? You'll have years to get to know these idiots. Let's focus on each other right now."

"Goth-boy, stop complaining. It's so not sexy."

"What is sexy?"

She giggled and shook her head. "Fishing for compliments is also not sexy."

"Did I tell you about the art studio the elementals are building for you? It will be right off the end of our wing on the second floor, and have sky lights. Stealth and I are wiring the windows to work off an app on your phone so you can open as many as you want with just the swipe of your finger."

"Now that is hot," she stepped into his body and wrapped her arms around him.

"Better than flowers?"

"Who wants flowers? Art is forever."

"So this is hot?"

"Definitely hot."

"Hot enough to get you to go back to bed?" Aquos pressed his lips to her pulse.

"After dinner," she slipped away from him. Her laughter was enough to make him smile, even as he reluctantly followed her down the hall. This family dinner was at Sally's command. She was excited M.J. had agreed to live with them full-time now, but he didn't see why he had to share her. He finally had something or rather someone of his own. He really hated being expected to share so soon. He smiled when he caught M.J. staring at one of the elemental's vases in a niche. She had that far-away from here look again. This was when he realized he would always have to share his woman, for she had a universe in her mind.

"What is this?"

"The elementals use them to document our history."

"But this is the only art from your world in the entire building. Why is that?"

"We'll have yours, soon."

"Your people don't do painting? Or sculpture?"

"The elementals prefer to focus on practical items."

"No, honey. You're wrong."

"What do you mean?"

"This is gorgeous." She picked up the piece with gentle hands, turning it to the light. The porcelain was so delicate, you could see the light through it. The notches creating an almost hypnotic effect as M.J. turned it under her examination. "I think this is art, their kind. How do you read it?"

"You'll learn all about our people, soon enough. Tonight is about family."

"Speaking of which … you met Squirt. She fully approves of you. Do you have any family I'll need the nod from?"

"The nod? I know this term not, my love."

"You know. The nod of approval. I'm not exactly the type of girl most families would be happy to see added to their tree."

"I'm water and you, my heart, are amazing. There are no trees involved."

"Family trees, goth-boy. Most people wouldn't be pleased to see me added."

"You humans have such humorous interests."

"Not answering my question, goth-boy."

He stopped them in their tracks as he looked deep in her eyes. "M.J. Storm … are you actually worried about this?"

"I just—"

Aquos brushed a kiss across her lips, and then in the center of each of her flaming cheeks. "You and I, my heart, are one. No male or female for that matter would ever stand between us. Push aside these fears please." When she started to open her mouth to argue with him, he kissed her again. "For the record, as I explained to you once, my sire perished shortly after we arrived. There are no others for my clan. I am the last of my kind."

"Right. That's what Gabriellele said."

"When did the archangel tell you that?"

"I … I don't remember." She shook her whole body, as if trying to dispel a web from her mind. "I'm so sorry about your family—"

He put his hand over her lips. "He was ill before we went through the portal, love. The devastation had affected his mind, and he was … unreachable to reason. Losing him was a good thing. Luke and Drake were there for me, I swear it. There is no reason for your sorrow, this was thousands of years ago, so you are truly safe from being denied access to my … tree, as you called it."

"Good." They kissed again.

"However, Sally did teach us one human custom I think is wise." Aquos knelt before M.J. and took her hand. The ring in his fist had been procured from Tamar; it belonged to the Water Clan's and had been placed in the vaults.

"Goth-boy, you know I'm yours."

"My understanding is this declares it for all to see. Please wear my clan's ring and declare our union for all to see. You already have my heart and everything of worth in my soul; I desire you to take this as well."

She sobbed and nodded. "There's a line from an old book I love. Make my happiness, and I will make yours."

"You already have, my M.J. You already have." Their lips came together and bodies fused with the joy of the moment. He hoped M.J. was actually reconsidering attending Sally's demanded family meeting when they both identified the sound of knocking on the front door. "We should get that. The elementals are surely preoccupied with dinner." She groaned when they separated and Aquos began to hope they could get out of the dinner after all.

They went together. Mostly because Aquos was unwilling to let her go for even the amount of time it would take to get to the front door, open it, and return to her side. Somehow it felt as if his body was still stuck on that beach, watching M.J. disappear into the silver flash of the lightning's strike. He gave her another squeeze before he reached for the doorknob.

When he saw who was on the other side, he gasped.

Squirt yelled, "The bastard sold the track and I need some place to live. It's your turn to save me," before she threw her body into M.J.'s' embrace, making her stagger several steps away from him.

He closed his eyes as he remembered his father's favorite saying. No matter what … always remember … the tides will turn.

All he could hope was they changed for the better.

 EPILOGUE

Keva watched the stranger stalking through the woods from a distance. Another one. The clan lords had gotten sloppy over the years and stopped watching their borders. Even the Elementals, so joyous to be free from their stasis were acting neglectful. Keva understood Luke and the dragon queen was trying to change things for the Omega, all of the Omega. It just wasn't happening fast enough. There were problems everywhere and she had no one she could go to. Scout clan take care of Scout clan, to hells with Luke's new orders.

Turning back toward her people, she froze as she re-lived in her mind her last plea to them. She had actually begged they stopped what they were doing. She tried to make them understand there might be another solution. It did not work.

She didn't belong with them anymore. They were making that abundantly clear.

Her problem was she didn't seem to belong anywhere.

She'd spent so much time with the clan lords since the holiday celebration a few months before. Dividing her days between the grand house and the Scout camp had left her feeling like she didn't belong in either. Keva had even moved her encampment away from the stream where the rest of her people were living, finding a small brook to use instead for her water.

The forest provided all else.

It just could not give companionship.

* * *

The architect moved through the trees, determined to get back to the creek's base. It came bubbling out of the ground just a few steps from the property boundaries, and then ambled through the forest surrounding Sanctuary's gates. His plans were to take out the Clan Lords inside the house, but the scouts refused to go inside so he had to take different measures.

A crystal vial held the green powder that, when sprinkled onto the water, turned it muddy for a moment, before the movement of the creek mixed the substances together. It would slowly erode their minds until they took the action he couldn't.

One was a meager force against so many in the Scout Clan.

Cautiously making his way back to his base, he paused when he heard someone screaming from inside the mansion. He had no idea what had moved into the house, but it sounded like nothing had prepared the Clan Lords for its arrival.

Just as they had no idea what they were dealing with when they had created him.

ARTEMIS MILCHON

 Artemis is a time-traveling princess from a distant planet. She spent her childhood hopping worm-holes across the galaxy. Fluent in one hundred and seventy - nine languages, only one of them from Earth, she learned to speak English from a man made out of metal. Her traveling companion is a fire-breathing kitten who is also a gourmet cook. Love and romance are her passion, and she's thrilled to share it with you. Come and join her for a tale or two ... we promise the kitty won't set you ablaze.

Keep watch for more stories from Artemis